A RAVE FOR IVY!

For Love of Ivy

A novel by
Carol Sturm
Smith

based on the screenplay
by Robert Alan Aurthur

from a story by Sidney Poitier

AN AVON BOOK

AVON BOOKS
A division of
The Hearst Corporation
959 Eighth Avenue
New York, New York 10019

First Printing, June, 1968
Fifth Printing, September, 1968

Cover design by Dick Smith

Printed in the U.S.A.

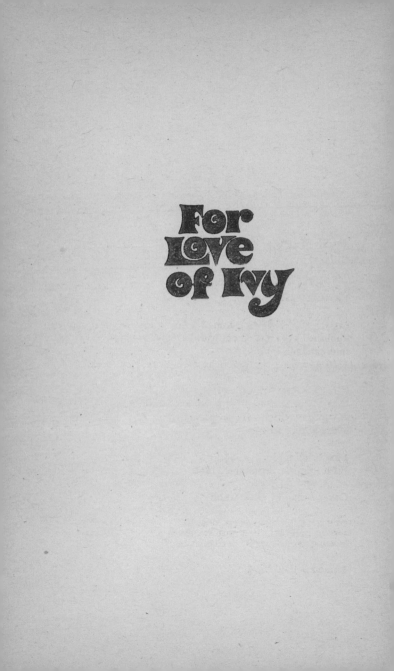

For Love of Ivy

Chapter One

Ivy lingered in the comfort of the warm water long after the second soaping had washed away. She left the shower reluctantly. The dawn clatter of the birds had wakened her from a restless sleep and she stretched to relieve the tensions in her lower back. The steam mist on the mirror cleared while Ivy adjusted her white full-slip straps, pulling them tight against her smooth, dark skin.

She pulled a brush irritably through her hair. The pretty face reflected in the mirror showed the lack of sleep around her eyes and mouth.

Silently she cursed her hair, impatient; it took a long time to catch up the stray ends and pin them back severely from her face. Finally, she smoothed on red lipstick and buttoned up her starched white uniform.

Through the window over her dresser Ivy watched the gardener walk along the path from the Austins' Long Island Sound frontage, past the swimming pool and pool house. The early morning dew glistened in the thin sunlight; the early morning sounds were hollow and separate and distinct.

She made the bed and dusted.

The story of my life in the North, Ivy thought, looking at the restaurant ashtrays that spotted the top of her dresser, listening to the rustle of her uniform loud in her ears. Ivy pressed a hand against her stomach. She didn't know the word for it . . . this feeling. A discontent . . . an *ache*—it sat on her liver like a rock-hard cold dumpling. The gardener placed the sprinklers over the lawn and headed for the front of the house out of sight.

The muted sounds of movement drifted down from upstairs: the Austins were awake. It was time to get started. And it was time to do something about the ache, too. Today, she thought. I'll tell her today.

". . . a terrible drag, luv. He never stopped moving at me all night. Don't you hate wet lips?" Gena sipped her orange juice and shifted her weight against the wall. "Of course I brushed him. . . . Tonight? Well, Freddy said something about driving up to his father's farm till Monday morning. He took his

8

new wife to London for a week." She laughed softly into the phone. "The father, luv, not Freddy."

She glanced at her parents, buried in their newspapers around the breakfast table, eating silently. Ivy hovered in the background, refilling the coffee cups.

Gena plucked a blond hair from the front of her dress and dropped it on the floor. "Sure, if you want to go," she said. "There'll be Terry and Ed and some couple from the city I don't know, and maybe Freddy's kid brother who I think is AWOL from the army."

Ivy cleared the juice glasses from the table. Frank was carefully reading the buyers arrival list, his finger keeping his place in the small type. Doris signalled for more coffee.

Through the sink window Ivy saw Tim leave the pool house and amble across the lawn, sandals flapping, dark glasses shading his eyes from the sunlight. He ignored a sprinkler, brushed his tangled hair off his forehead with one hand and arrived in the kitchen with his rumpled blue workshirt and dirty khakis damp from the spray. He rested the cup of coffee Ivy handed him on the counter, lit a cigarette and coughed hoarsely.

Frank glanced up. "Doris, I thought he ran away from home," he said with distaste.

Doris lowered her newspaper. "He got as far as the pool house." She wrinkled her nose against an imagined smell.

"If it weren't for the sprinklers he'd never get water on him!" Frank glowered at his son.

Tim rolled his eyes high, gulped his coffee and handed the cup to Ivy. "Coming home for dinner?" she asked him softly. "I'll make you a pot roast."

Tim nodded. "Yeah. Later." He loped out of the kitchen, deliberately slapping his sandals against the floor. Ivy smiled helplessly at the look on Frank's face and quickly turned back to the sink. The squeal of Tim's motorcycle accelerating drowned out the sound of running water. Frank rustled his newspaper and shifted his weight in the chair.

Gena signalled for more coffee and Ivy carried the pot over to the phone. Gena gulped her coffee. "Okay, twelve thirty, see you then." She hung up the phone. "Won't be home for dinner," Gena called to Ivy, and followed her father who had made a sudden exit. Doris neatly folded her newspaper, finished her coffee and moved slowly after them.

Ivy took a deep breath. It'll be even harder tomorrow, she told herself. Her lips firm with determination, she caught up with Doris in the hall and stationed herself at the front door.

"Mrs. Austin. . ."

Chapter Two

"Ivyyyy! Noooo!"

"What the hell!" Frank stopped short at his wife's shriek. "Gena, get my car out," he said to his daughter and walked briskly back to the house. Doris and Ivy were in the kitchen.

"Doris, what's the *matter?*" he demanded.

"Frank, Ivy says she's leaving." Doris's shoulders were slumped and she was obviously upset. Her fingers toyed with the small pearl cluster on her right ear.

Ivy nodded in agreement and lowered her eyes. Doris wailed at Frank's shrug. "Frank, she can't just leave her family."

"Sure . . ." he agreed. Doris seemed reasonable. "Not just like that."

"It's true, Mr. Austin. You *have* been like a family to me. . . ."

"*Like* a family?" Disbelief hardered Doris's voice. "You *are* family." Her face brightened and she grew animated. "Ivy, I know what you really mean. You want to take your vacation now, to go to Florida and see your folks. That's fine with us." She looked at Frank and nudged him with her elbow.

"No problem!" he agreed quickly. "We'll fly you down and back. Take as long as you want. A week, ten days. . ." His voice trailed off weakly at the vigorous shake of Ivy's head.

"There's none of my folks left in Florida." Her voice was flat. She looked away. A spot of dried orange juice clung to the top of the formica serving table and Ivy dampened a sponge at the sink.

Doris was thinking hard. "Well, we'll send you anywhere else you want to go." She got a sudden thought. "Africa?" she asked quizzically.

Ivy dabbed the spot away and replaced the sponge under the sink. She turned to face them. "I want to move into the city, Mrs. Austin." It was final, she thought. I am not going to change my mind. She tightened her lips and stood her ground.

"You have another job," Doris said suspiciously. Her voice was angry when Ivy didn't answer. "I knew it! Judy Townsend. Came up here last Tuesday night, stole you right from under my nose. I'll kill her!"

"It's not the Townsends. . . ." Ivy protested.

Doris ignored her denial with a small wave of her hand. "Did Judy Townsend offer you a job or didn't she?"

"She's *always* offering me a job."

Doris looked at Frank triumphantly. "I knew it! I'll kill her!"

She began pacing the floor, arms crossed in front of her, searching for a solution to the dilemma. She waved off Frank's arm irritably—how could he be so impatient at a time like this!

Frank turned to Ivy. "If it's a matter of money . . ."

"Not money." She shook her head slowly in emphasis.

"Too much work?"

"I'll increase the people for the heavy cleaning to three times a week," Doris offered quickly.

"It's not the work," Ivy said positively.

"Then what?" Frank asked. His voice was gentle and Ivy realized that he was honestly curious. But she didn't answer. . . . She didn't even know for sure herself.

"Frank, wait in the car for me," Doris gave him an easy push. "I'll be a few minutes."

He moved slowly to the door. "I'm sure we can

13

work something out," he muttered as he left the kitchen.

Doris motioned Ivy to sit. "Have a cup of coffee with me. Please."

Ivy shook her head. "Could we talk while I work, ma'am?"

"Of course."

Ivy headed for the carpeted stairs with Doris at her heels, talking into her back. "You know, nine years ago when we found you in Florida, you were an innocent . . ." she groped for words before continuing ". . . an innocent, scrawny eighteen-year-old, ignorant in the ways of the world. . . ."

"And nine years later I'm no longer scrawny." Ivy headed for the Austins' bedroom, pausing at the hall closet to pick up a vacuum cleaner which she dropped on the bedroom floor.

"I figure if I'm in the city I can get my high school diploma," Ivy explained. "Then go on to secretarial school." She quickly stripped the bed.

"But I started to say, Ivy, that it took me exactly one week to discover you were a gem. And then, remember——" Doris looked around her. "Where do you keep the clean sheets?"

"The hall closet. I'll get them all later."

"Anyway, remember how I went right to your grandmother and aunt and asked if they'd consider letting you come north with us?"

"That was the best news they'd ever had, ma'am,"

Ivy said, piling the dirty clothes in a corner with the sheets.

"You keep calling me ma'am, and I keep wanting to tell you to call me 'Doris,' like my friends," Doris said in a wheedling voice, "Or 'Mother' like Gena and Tim." She made a gesture of disgust as Frank's automobile horn bleated shrilly from the driveway.

Ivy knew with a sudden clarity that she had made the right decision. She picked up the vacuum cleaner and moved into Doris's workroom, pursued by her coaxing. Ivy left the vacuum at the door and began pushing the crumpled papers that littered the floor into the wastepaper basket. She replaced several volumes in the well-stocked bookshelves and emptied the overflowing ashtrays. Ivy noticed that Doris's suit was copied from a rough sketch taped to the wall over the drawing board; several new sketches of the suit, with the sleeves tapered slightly and the jacket shortened, were on the board.

Doris, trying to be helpful, had finally located the vacuum cleaner's self-storing cord and she tugged at it gingerly. "Where does this go?"

"The plug's in the floor under your drafting table," Ivy pointed.

"Oh, of course." She pulled the cleaner across the floor by the cord.

"The fact I want to leave doesn't mean I don't love all of you, ma'am," Ivy tried to explain. "But there's nothing here for me." She cut off Doris's protest with

15

a wave. "I mean, you've got Mr. Austin, Gena, Tim, your work. . . ." She paused and searched for the words. "But I look ahead and I don't see *any* of that."

Doris was bending over, looking for the floor plug. "What happened to that nice young man who worked for the gas company?"

"That was two years ago. He married a college girl."

The phone rang and Doris sprang at the opportunity to drop the vacuum cord, narrowly missing the drafting table with her head. She reached the phone before Ivy.

"Hello. . . . Who? . . . I'm sorry, Mr. Hults, but you must have the wrong——"

"That's the plumber," Ivy interrupted, reaching for the phone. "Hello, Mr. Hults, this is Ivy. Well, I've been having a problem with my dishwasher. . . ."

The Austin house in King's Point was a rambling, modern gem of stone and glass, isolated from its neighbors by an almost solid hedge of rambling roses, Russian olive and silver bell which grew between well-spaced trees. The driveway forked around the house, and Frank stood now on the gravel next to the car which Gena had pulled out of the garage. His toe kicked small bits of stone and dust into the air; the sun hurt his eyes, and it was late and he was fuming. Gena sat on the low wall separating the driveway from the expanse of green lawn. Her head was thrown back, eyes shut, the sun warm against her face.

"This is ridiculous," Frank said suddenly, moving to the edge of the grass. Gena looked up: Doris was walking briskly along the path to the pool house, following Ivy who was carrying clean bedding over her right arm.

"Doris!" Frank yelled. His hands pushed hard into his sides over his belt.

"In a minute, Frank," she yelled over her shoulder.

Ivy opened the door of the pool house and went in, but Doris stopped on her heels. "Ugh! I can't even *look* in there."

"In a way he has his own system," Ivy explained, glancing around at the mess. The sheets on the couch Tim used as a bed were rumpled into a ball, more on the floor than not. Ivy tossed them near the door and looked around in vain for some dirty clothes. In one corner Tim had stacked his scuba gear and a collection of old racing magazines, but there his attempt at neatness had ended: cigarette butts and spent matches dotted the floor between piles of books and magazine clippings and several dozen records, all out of their jackets.

Doris took a few tentative steps into the room and tripped on an empty beercan. "Ugh!" She shuddered and backed up to the door.

"Doris, *now*," they heard Frank yell.

"I said in a minute, Frank," Doris shot back and

turned around. Frank had planted himself across the pool, his arms akimbo, a dangerously angry look on his face.

"I'll be right back, Ivy." Her heels clicked on the concrete.

"Doris, what's the problem?" His voice had the icy ring of barely controlled fury.

"Ivy wants to leave," she said as if that should explain it sufficiently.

"I know Ivy wants to leave," he said, throwing up his hands. "But what's the *problem?*"

"Well . . ." Doris broke off.

"Well, nothing!" Frank raised his voice and Gena, who was walking toward them, quickened her pace. "We have a maid who wants to quit, so we get *another* maid." Frank was yelling now.

"Daddy, ssshh!" Gena interrupted, looking toward the pool house, embarrassed.

"Don't shush me!" Frank yelled. He lowered his voice and turned back to Doris. "In fact," he continued, "we get three maids. You pick up the phone, dial the employment agency, and say, 'Send over eighty-two candidates,' out of which you pick eleven if you want them."

"That simple," Doris said sarcastically.

"Of course that simple." Frank folded his arms on his chest and looked smugly from his wife to his daughter.

"And so, another little problem is solved," Gena

18

chimed in sweetly, saccharine dripping from her voice.

"Any objections?" Frank asked suspiciously. He had the feeling that he was about to be attacked and he steeled himself.

"Doesn't it matter to you she's like a member of the family?" Gena raised her own voice.

"How do you suggest I express my grief?"

"Would you be so cavalier if I calmly announced one morning I was leaving?" Gena shot back.

"Just try me," he said to her harshly. "My dear daughter, what you don't seem to realize is that, even though Ivy's been with us seven years——"

"Nine years," Doris corrected.

"——*Nine* years, and though we may all adore her, she wants to leave, and there's *nothing we can do about it!*"

"Well, she can't leave." Doris said positively.

"Tell me why she can't leave," Frank asked his wife patiently, as if he were talking to a child.

"Because," she told her husband icily, "two weeks from tomorrow, *I* am going on the buying trip to Europe. *I* have to bring back all our next year's lines, and *I*, as you have very often pointed out, am solely responsible for twenty-two point six per cent of our yearly volume." Doris's voice was shrill.

"So?" he yelled, ignoring Gena's tug at his sleeve.

"So, in addition to a nine-year personal relationship,

I can't leave without someone responsible to run the house."

"Somehow, I have the feeling we'll survive." Frank drew out the words. "Maybe just barely, but——"

"Oh, *Frank*. . . ." Doris wailed, exasperated.

They stared at each other in frustrated silence—dead end. Gena saw Ivy exit from the pool house. She called out and Ivy waited for her to catch up.

"It's nothing I've done, is it?" Gena was genuinely upset.

"Of course not, Gena," she said gently. "Look . . . please don't make this any tougher. It's taken me three days to get up the nerve as it is, girl." Ivy smiled wryly.

"Okay . . . Sure." Gena nodded her head.

"And it's not like I'm never going to hear from you again. I mean, you're going to call me at least five times a week, because I've got to know the latest on Freddy, Lenny, Jay, Jonathan, Bruce, Dick and Larry."

Gena grinned. "You left out Peter," she said.

Ivy's laughter trickled away as she looked up and saw the pained expression on Doris's face across the pool.

Ivy left the dirty sheets on the path and walked around the pool. "I'm sorry, Mrs. Austin, but . . ." Ivy looked over at Frank and back to Doris. "What if another nine years go by, nice and easy like the last, and I'm past thirty-five and I still have nothing?" She got the words out in a rush and knew before Doris answered that she hadn't understood at all—not at all. She had a sinking feeling in her stomach.

"Nothing!" Doris exclaimed, looking hurt. "Ivy, you have a good home, people who care for you. . . . A good job!"

"I don't think Ivy's talking about those things, Doris," Frank interrupted.

"It's not any of that," Ivy agreed. "In the city I'll have a chance. At least I have to *try*."

"Try for what? What do you want?" Doris asked.

"I'm not sure," Ivy answered. "I just know . . . I haven't got it now."

Doris looked hopelessly defeated as Ivy walked slowly back to the house, retrieving the sheets on the way. She'll never understand, Ivy thought. All she can see is that I'm a maid and maids are supposed to keep things orderly and not rock the boat.

Well, the boat was rocking and Ivy felt just a little bit seasick. But seasickness never killed anyone—it was a strictly temporary disability.

Chapter Three

Austin's Department Store was in a suburban shopping complex, an easy drive from King's Point. Over the years it had built up a clientele who preferred ample parking space and ease of shopping to the inconvenience and noise of Manhattan. On one of the heavy glass main doors, discreetly lettered in gold paint, was the store's motto:

Courtesy Is Our Middle Name
Quality Our Family Tradition

The window displays were changed twice a month, except during each December when they were occupied by two Santas who held court to long lines of waiting parents whose small children were presented with an inexpensive toy and a helium-filled balloon reading: *Austin's*.

To the right of the main entrance, across from Men's Furnishings, brightly colored streamers hung to the floor from a sign that read: GENA'S BOUTIQUE. The space had been occupied by the store photographer until Gena had persuaded her parents to set up the shop. It had proved to be an excellent move: in less than six months the Boutique was showing a healthy profit; it had become a hang-out of sorts where customers were offered coffee and cheese from a serve-yourself buffet.

Now Gena was standing with Freddy and her friend Sandy. Sandy had tried on a mini-dress and was doing a series of turns in front of a three-way mirror. Freddy was feeling rambunctious, and kept up a steady stream of comment about Sandy's posturing: Gena was laughing hopelessly.

"Gena!"

She turned. Tim was beckoning to her from the back of the Boutique, partially obscured from view by an arrangement of Carnaby Street posters. Gena signalled a salesgirl to take over and eluded Freddy's attempt to pat her on the rear.

"Please don't grope the help, Freddy. Be right back, Sandy."

"I like it," Sandy said suddenly. "But don't you think it's a bit long, Freddy?"

Gena laughed and quickly crossed the Boutique to Tim.

"Who·let you out?" The motorcycle ride to the store had added a thin patina of new dirt to his clothes.

"Never mind that, man," he said to her. "What's with Mom? She's got the vapors. Says she's not going on the Paris trip."

"Ivy's quitting," Gena told him sadly.

"You're putting me on!" He didn't believe it.

Gena shook her head.

"That's the worst! Why?" he wailed.

"She wants to go . . . out there."

"What's out there?"

"Secretarial school, a career, love, marriage, family. . . ." Gena shrugged her shoulders.

"She wants the mainstream?" Tim ran his hand through his tangled hair.

"In no uncertain terms."

"We can't let her!" he said positively. "First off, if Ivy got out from between me and Dad . . . he might . . . enlist me in the Army!" Ivy leaving—it was unthinkable!

Tim looked at Gena hopefully, as if she might have a solution to the problem. He took her arm urgently. "Listen, we've gotta talk about this."

"Well, not here," Gena snapped. She started back across the Boutique, heading for the shipping department at the rear of the store. Tim stopped to look at

Sandy, who had changed into an even shorter mini-dress.

"Stop drooling!" Gena said.

"Establishment-oriented chicks don't interest me except as a social comment for my book," Tim said righteously. "I can't stand it here," he added suddenly.

"Why don't you quit?" Gena asked him.

"Why don't you get me her phone number?"

Gena's face screwed up; the thought was too outlandish to even consider. They left the Boutique and Tim turned his attention back to the problem at hand.

"If she wants to go to secretarial school, she can go right across the street here at night," he suggested.

Gena shook her head. "She insists on moving into the city."

"But why?"

"How would *I* know why?" Gena said sharply.

Tim shrugged and pushed against a set of double doors, holding them open for Gena in a rare burst of thoughtfulness.

The shipping department opened on the rear of Austin's Department Store. A fully-loaded truck with a PAR-TAL TRUCKING sign on its side was just pulling out from the loading area, making room for another Par-Tal truck to move in.

The men working on the loading platform whistled appreciatively as Gena greeted them on her way to the soda machine. She passed beneath a large sign, in bright day-glo colors with a psychedelic border:

AUSTIN SHIPPING DEPARTMENT
TIMOTHY AUSTIN, PROP.

She got two cokes, walked back, handed one to Tim and perched on a box, her skirt pulled well up her thighs.

"All right, guys," Tim ordered, "you've all seen Gena naked before." The men guffawed and went back to work.

"It just occurred to me this whole thing might come down to the one big difference between you and Ivy," Tim said thoughtfully.

"What's color got to do with it?" Gena asked, surprised.

"Not color," he explained. "But wherever you are eleven guys are looking to make you. Maybe it's that simple. Maybe she only needs a guy to romance her a little." He lit a cigarette and waited for Gena's reaction.

"I assumed Ivy was pretty well taken care of in that department," Gena said slowly after a pause. She crossed her legs to avoid a sharp edge of wood.

"But when did she last have a *proper* date?" he asked.

"I don't know." Gena was thinking—she really didn't know.

"It's easy for you." Tim said. "Guys hang around here, or drive to the house, sit around, drink the old man's scotch. You've got more action than you can use."

"She goes into the city on her days off," Gena mused.

"So what does she do there?"

"I don't know," Gena answered truthfully.

"Do you tell her what you do?"

Gena nodded.

"But she doesn't tell you what she does?" Tim asked.

Gena shook her head again.

"Then maybe she doesn't do anything!" Tim brushed his hair back from his forehead.

"But what can we do about it?" Gena asked.

Tim ground his cigarette out against the stone floor and rubbed the back of his hand against his mouth. "What if we line her up with a guy?" he said finally.

"Like who?" It was an idea worth considering.

Tim paced a small circle in front of the box, the noise of the trucks and the men working sounding loud in his ears. A heavy truck door slammed closed and an engine turned over. He looked at Gena and shook his head slowly, his mouth set in a thin line, unable to summon up a single suggestion.

"I'm afraid my friends wouldn't qualify either," Gena said softly.

"Damn right," Tim snapped. "None of them good enough."

They were silent for a long time, mulling it over. Tim's mind was blank as he watched the loading activity further out on the platform. A Par-Tal truck backed in and the very fat Negro driver got down from the cab of the truck, heading for the ramp.

"Hey! There's an idea. . . ." The excitement in his voice startled Gena. She looked over at the platform as Tim headed away. "Not *him!*" She wailed, horrified.

"Just cool it," Tim called over his shoulder. Gena jumped up and followed him, cursing as she snagged a stocking on the rough wood.

Tim intercepted the driver. "Hey, man . . ."

"Mr. Austin?"

"Where're your bosses?"

"Guess they're at the office." Tim nodded his thanks and the driver walked on over to the shipping department checker and handed over his manifests.

Tim turned to Gena. "Give me some change."

"What are you going to do?" Gena dug in her purse, and followed Tim to the wall phone.

"What we need is a cat who's real safe. A swinger, but a bum. . . ." Tim peered over to the Par-Tal truck and dialed the number on the sign.

"No!" Gena protested.

"A cat we can control," Tim continued. "Someone who'll wine and dine her but won't marry her. A good-looking nogoodnik."

Gena frowned her disapproval.

"Par-Tal Trucking? This is Mr. Austin of Austin's Inc. I'd like to speak to Mr. Parks or Mr. Talbot."

While he waited Tim quickly explained the rest of

the plan to Gena. "All you have to do is have Ivy here around like two thirty. It'll all look like an accident to her, but I'll set this guy up."

"You can't use the business to blackmail a man," Gena protested.

"Will you just get Ivy here!" Tim quickly turned back to the phone.

"Oh, good morning, Parks," he said, deepening his voice. "This is Mr. Austin. I was wondering if you were free to run up here for a little late lunch. . . ."

Jack Parks eased his car into the Austin shipping area and headed for the front of the store, an attache case held loosely in his right hand. He walked past the Par-Tal truck with pleasure. A driver called: "Hey, boss. Come to spy on us?"

Jack waved. "Lunch with Mr. Austin. We're thinking of buying the place." The driver laughed appreciatively and dug an elbow into his helper's side.

The thin leather soles of Jack's shoes made little sound as he walked through the store, heading for the restaurant in the basement. He stopped and checked his tie and straightened the jacket of his custom-made suit in a mirror before going down the stairs. The restaurant was almost empty and he ran his eyes quickly around the room looking for Frank Austin. He wasn't there, but Tim was peering over the back of a booth, gesturing to him. What the hell does *he* want? Jack skirted a table of dessert pastries and headed over.

My God, Tim thought, why didn't I think of Par-Tal right away! This here is one handsome black cat —and he moves like a goddamn athlete. Ivy will *flip*.

"Sit down, man," Tim said, thoroughly pleased with himself.

"Where's your father?"

Tim sipped from the glass he held in his hand. "He didn't phone you. I did."

Jack looked at him thoughtfully before sitting down.

"Whatever you want to eat, I'll get it for you," Tim said.

"Maybe just some of that iced tea." Jack looked at Tim's shirt with disgust. This is some raggedy-ass kid, he thought.

Tim waved for the waitress and ordered the iced tea. "So how've you been?" he asked.

"Fine," Jack said broadly. "I was fine Monday night when you saw me, and I'm fine now."

"Monday night. Yeah . . . wow!" Tim toyed with his glass and took a sip of his iced tea.

"You're not married, are you?" Tim asked him.

"No." He wished Tim would get to the point.

"Nice-looking guy like you," Tim continued. "You're obviously not up-tight for bread." Tim took another sip of his drink, looking at Jack across the top of the glass. "You're not . . . you know?" He made an effeminate gesture with his hand.

"No, I'm not!" Jack said. He fought down a strong

impulse to empty the tea in Tim's hand over his un-kempt head.

"Can't hardly tell these days," Tim said quickly. "We got a guy designs chicks' clothes, floats off his toes, you know?" Jack gave no reaction. "He's got a wife and four kids. On the other hand, I've got a karate instructor—the freak of the world."

"You get me up here for a sociological discussion?" Jack looked at his watch.

Tim shook his head and pushed his hair back from his eyes. He nervously lit a cigarette.

"You owe us money?" Jack asked him finally.

"You know I'm strictly cash, man."

"Then what *did* you get me here for?" Jack could feel his impatience rising to the surface and he forced himself to remain calm.

Tim flicked the ash off the end of his cigarette, missing the ashtray. He looked around for the wait-ress and fidgeted in his chair. "We've got a maid named Ivy. I want you to take her out."

Tim had timed it perfectly; just then the waitress arrived with Jack's tea. "Oh, my check, baby," Tim said brightly.

Jack didn't know whether to laugh at Tim or hit him, so he got up and walked to the dessert table. Tim followed him eagerly, holding the check.

"I think while I'm here I will talk to your father," Jack said. "You should be put away, man. I worked till five thirty this morning, then had to go to the of-

31

fice at eight because two drivers are out sick. My partner, *Prince* Talbot, refuses to get up in the morning, so half our deliveries are late."

He deliberated for a minute, and finally chose two Danish from the tray. Tim handed the waitress his check and followed Jack back to the table.

"What I'm telling you, man," Jack said, stopping suddenly, "is that this trip was *not* necessary."

He sat down at the table and bit savagely into a Danish. Tim sensed an advantage and he grinned.

"You'll like her," he said positively.

Jack stared at Tim, his mouth full of pastry, and burst out laughing at the absurdity of Tim telling him what he would like. Tim cautiously joined in the laughter.

"What makes you think I'd make a good stud?" Jack asked him.

"Aren't all . . . uh . . . *you* superior at that kind of thing?"

Jack's laughter died; he was no longer amused. Ye gods, he thought, I should have known better.

"Know something, hippy?" he snarled angrily. "Boss's son or no boss's son, the next move you get your teeth pushed down into your toes."

Tim plucked a flower from a vase on the table and offered it to him. "How could you zap a flower child?"

He was too much! Jack tapped his fingers on the

table. "Sonny, shouldn't you be wrapping packages instead of procuring for colored domestics?"

"This is a special case," Tim explained. "She wants to quit, after nine years."

"So let her leave."

"Impossible," Tim said.

Jack looked around the dining room furtively, then leaned across the table. "I got news, Mr. Charlie," he said. "Slavery's been abolished."

Tim slouched forward in his chair and rested his arms on the table, an intent, persuasive look coming over his face. "All I ask is you meet a girl," he said.

"You said you want me to take her out."

"Just meet her," Tim begged.

"Why me?" O Lord, why me? he thought.

"It would have been your partner Talbot if he'd answered the phone," Tim told him honestly.

"Billy has no compunctions about zapping weekend hippies," Jack told him.

"Then I'm lucky it's you." Tim played with his glass, lit another cigarette, finished his iced tea and then tried to explain the situation. "See, Ivy *thinks* she wants to get married, but what she really needs is a little basic fulfillment, a little id-exercise . . ."

"You've discussed this with her?" Jack asked. His foot began tapping the floor lightly under the table.

Tim shook his head. "Listen, man, I may have majored in merchandising at Cornell before I dropped out, but my minor was in psychology. Also, I've had three years of my own analysis. Nobody has to fill me in on that scene. You fit the bill. You obviously aren't married because you have problems of your own—and, besides, you're a sort of a shady character."

Jack swallowed down his iced tea and got up, retrieving his attache case from the seat.

" 'Bye," he said.

Tim got up hurriedly, fumbled in his pocket for some change and came up empty handed.

"Mind leaving the tip?" he asked.

Jack shook his head in disgust, dropped some change on the table and headed for the door, following Tim past the cashier.

"Sorry, Tim," she said. "Orders from your father. Strictly cash."

Tim looked helplessly at Jack. Jack clenched his teeth, dug two singles out of his pocket, dropped them on the cashier's tray and walked off. Tim pocketed the change.

They walked back along the corridor to the stairs which led to the main floor.

"What's your first name, by the way?" Tim asked him.

"Jack."

"I always think of you as Par of Par-Tal."

"When you're not thinking of me as that uppity black with the trucks, you mean." Jack was thoroughly annoyed.

"I love you, man," Tim said indignantly. "Why are you so hostile?"

Jack looked at Tim before answering. "Damned if I know," he said finally. The kid just annoyed him.

They had reached the stairs.

"Another thing," Jack said. "*How* did you figure to get me to do this?" He was curious.

"By appealing to your better nature?" Tim said, tentatively, trying to find the key.

Jack shook his head with a little snort.

"Racial togetherness?"

Jack frowned. Strike two.

"Then how about exposure?"

"Exposure?" The word sent an icy chill down his backbone.

"Well, I've got this square friend who writes for the Daily *News,*" Tim explained. "It came to me you'd make a groovy subject for a piece. Your *whole* trucking operation—you know, how it got started, what you developed it into . . ." he looked to see how Jack was responding. "The *whole* thing."

Jack stared at him. "You wouldn't do that." He might, he thought, this lousy kid just might.

"The publicity would be great. It's a fascinating story."

"You're a rotten kid!" Jack told him softly, his hand tightening around the attache case.

"I'm just trying to be helpful," Tim protested with

35

self-righteous glee. "I was a boy scout in my early adolescence."

"You're wasting your time, baby." Jack resisted an almost overpowering desire to push Tim flat on the seat of his dirty jeans and kick the smug smile off his face.

They had reached the top of the stairs and Tim chuckled with obvious delight, looking past Jack down the main corridor. "What do you know, man," he said softly. "A wild coincidence!"

Jack followed Tim's eyes slowly. He knew with an awful clarity that he was about to be had.

"Here's Ivy now," Tim was saying. "With my sister. Now it's no problem at all to meet her." He took Jack's arm and propelled him toward the girls. "Hey, Gena!" Tim called.

Gena waved at him. "Oh, Ivy, there's Tim," she said. She took Ivy under the arm and urged her forward. "And I *wonder* who that good-looking man is with him."

They merged in the aisle of Women's Shoes. "Hey, this is a surprise," Tim said to Gena.

"I talked Ivy into getting some shoes," Gena said, looking at Jack. She glanced her approval at Tim, pleasantly surprised.

"I don't *need* any shoes!" Ivy protested, glancing at Jack surreptitiously.

"Gena, this is Jack Parks. Jack, my sister Gena."

36

"How do you do?" he asked politely. O Lord, he thought, how did I get into this one?

"You're that marvelous Mr. Parks Tim is always talking about," Gena gushed, prodding Ivy. "You know, Ivy, the one with all the trucks."

"I never heard . . ." Ivy began to say.

"And this is Ivy Moore, Jack," Tim interrupted.

"How do you do, Miss Moore?" Jack asked. His voice was cool and impersonal.

"Fine, I'm sure." Ivy turned back to Gena. "I really don't need anything."

Jack picked up a frivolous shoe from the display table at his side. "I don't see how you can live without these," he said to Ivy, reading from the card. "Imported Italian Florentine Flats." He handed her the shoe.

Why is he so hostile? she wondered. Ivy returned the shoe to the table feeling surprisingly awkward. She glanced at him out of the corner of her eye. Tim grinned at Gena.

"Well, I guess I've got to . . ."

"*Listen*," Tim interrupted, forcing Jack to stop, "why don't we all go to the cafeteria and have a bite? I'm *starving*."

"So am I," Gena seconded eagerly.

"I just fed you lunch," Ivy said flatly, looking at her in surprise.

"Then I've got a better idea." Gena hastily changed her tactics. "As long as you're in the neighborhood,

Mr. Parks, why not come to the house for dinner? We'd love having you."

"I thought you weren't coming home for dinner," Ivy said.

"I just changed my mind."

"Hey, that's great," Tim blurted. "What's for dinner, Ivy?"

Ivy glared at him. "I told you—pot roast."

"Groovy!" Tim exclaimed. "Jack, Ivy's pot roast is really out of sight."

"I'm not really fond of pot roast," he said stiffly.

"Neither am I," Tim agreed heartily.

In an awkward group they drifted out of Women's Shoes into Men's Furnishings. Tim grabbed Ivy by the arm and pulled her along to keep up with Jack. "Ivy, how about some of your fantastic bouillabaisse?" Tim asked, keeping an eye on Jack, ready to stop him if he headed for the door.

"Whatever you want." Ivy was puzzled. Tim asked her for pot roast at least three times a week.

"Bouillabaisse takes a long while, but with me helping . . ." Gena smiled innocently at Jack. "How's nine o'clock, Mr. Parks?"

Jack spotted a rack of ties and stopped to finger them. He glanced at Ivy. She seemed very ill at ease. Why, she might be attractive if she did something with her hair, he thought. He mellowed as he realized that she was the innocent bystander—she was being railroaded by Tim and Gena, too.

"Like the tie?" he asked her softly.

She ran her fingers over the material and looked at him carefully. "The striped one would look better with your suit," she told him.

Jack looked down and slowly replaced the tie on the rack. Well, well, he thought, she speaks her mind. He liked that.

"How's nine o'clock, Mr. Parks?" Gena walked over to the counter and leaned against it, looking up into his face.

And against his better judgment, Jack slowly nodded his acceptance. He turned away from Gena's smile of obvious satisfaction and started for Tim, a look of deliberation hardening his face. Putting an arm around Tim's shoulders, he forced him to stroll away, and leaning over so the girls behind them couldn't hear he hissed into Tim's ear: "I have the feeling, baby, you are going to be run over with a truck and then beaten up by a lot of colored people."

He let Tim shrug off his arm, frowned with distaste at the look of triumph on his face and walked out, ignoring Tim's outstretched hand.

Chapter Four

The Par-Tal Trucking garage, on the Queens side of the Midtown Tunnel, nestled between padlocked warehouses guarded by old night watchmen and modern burglar-alarm systems. It was a dreary, non-residential section of the borough, the stone and brick buildings grayed with the exhausts of industry and trucks, the windows opaque with accumulated grime. At rest for the night, empty trailer trucks silently lined the yard; a dim yellow light outlined the one Par-Tal truck backed up against the loading platform, the driver's door open. Eddie, Jack's chauffeur, sat in the limousine parked off to one side in the shadows; the big car looked decidedly out of place.

Jerry, a Negro in his early thirties, dressed in coveralls, stood easily by the truck noisily cracking his knuckles; the sound carried sharply in the early night stillness and Eddie closed his window in annoyance. Jerry checked his watch; they were getting a late start. He rotated his arms slowly, holding them straight out, shoulder high, loosening up his muscles.

It was a good ten minutes more before Jack's convertible turned into the yard and braked to a stop parallel to his limousine.

Jerry pulled himself up into the cab of the truck and started the engine. It turned over immediately and idled easily.

Jack sauntered over and gave Eddie instructions before heading for the passenger side of the truck. The limousine drove out of the lot, its headlight beams cutting through the gloom, momentarily catching Jack in the glare. He was dressed in coveralls and the crispness had gone out of his step. Tired . . . he was very tired, and it was an effort to keep his shoulders unslumped.

Jerry leaned across the cab and opened the passenger door for him, anxious to get started. Jack sank back against the seat, his eyes closed, as the heavy truck slithered out of the shipping platform dock. Jerry eased the truck onto the street, shifted the gears and waited.

"Where to, man?" he asked Jack finally.

"Get over to Northern Boulevard," Jack said. He didn't open his eyes, but he knew Jerry was waiting.

He wasn't going to like it. "I've arranged to be picked up somewhere in Great Neck."

"Not in Nassau!" Jerry exploded.

Jack nodded his head slowly.

"Do we have to?" Jerry knew that Jack was aware of the danger, but he said it anyway. "The state fuzz worry me."

Jack glanced over at him and put his feet up against the front of the cab. "A lot of things worry me, Jerry . . . so just go where I tell you!" He yawned, rearranged himself and settled back into the seat.

He was snoring gently, almost silently beneath the sounds of the truck and the traffic, before they reached the ramp leading to the Long Island Expressway.

The magenta-and-bright-orange optical designs first drew attention to the breast area and then to the small circle of material missing at the navel. Although not particularly short for a mini-dress, Ivy still thought it was outlandish—in the worst possible taste.

"It's *you,* Ivy," Gena said with conviction, thrusting it at her.

"I wouldn't be caught *dead* in it."

Gena had come barging into her room without knocking, the dress in her hand; *she* had already changed for dinner into a navy mini-dress with bright pink strips down the side and outlining the matching oval holes at her waist. She had pinned a small wiglet to the top of her head, arranging it into a curl that bounced when she walked. A small purse of large beads on a long chain rested lightly on her shoulder and she toyed with the catch.

Ivy headed for the kitchen in her slip when Gena snatched away the clean uniform she took from the closet, holding it behind her back as if she had stolen another child's lollipop. She offered the magenta horror instead.

"I'd look awful stupid in that thing," Ivy said over her shoulder.

Gena kept up her campaign, vigorously pleading and cajoling, digging up a surprising number of very plausible reasons why Ivy should at least try it on, moving around the kitchen like a gadfly, getting in Ivy's way. From time to time Ivy glanced at the clock. She ignored Gena as best she could while she finished the preparations for dinner.

The arguments had begun running to the absurd as Ivy carefully filled the deviled eggs through a pastry bag with a thin fluted tube, arranging them in clusters around the edge of the hors d'oeuvres tray. She stepped back, satisfied, and warded off Gena who quickly tried to take advantage of the opportunity.

"And if I had to serve dinner in that thing I'd sure feel stupid." She glared at Gena.

There was no mistaking the finality in Ivy's voice; the deliberate unnecessary slam of the refrigerator door. Gena fell silent, defeated at last, sullenly watching Ivy work at the stove.

Help with the dinner . . . *hah!* She's never cooked a meal in her *life*, Ivy thought, glancing over. Gena had slumped into a chair at the breakfast table. She tasted the soup and stirred in some salt. Tim's motorcycle turned into the driveway, heading for the garage.

"Now, let me get into my uniform." Gena handed it over reluctantly.

Ivy was fully dressed, back working at the stove when Tim burst into the kitchen.

"Man, what a pair!" he exclaimed to Gena, plopping down at the table. "When I left them, *he* was complaining he already saw the movie, and *she* didn't want to go to the club."

Ivy looked over suspiciously. "Your folks not coming home? I got enough dinner for ten people."

"That Jack Parks eats a lot." Tim winked at Gena.

"How come you have him to dinner?" Ivy asked.

"Business, man." Tim shrugged, grinning. "You don't know the problems I got with that shipping department."

"Since when did you care?" Ivy asked suspiciously.

Tim ignored her question. "I thought you were going to get her into some decent threads." He looked at Gena in annoyance.

She showed him the dress. "I tried."

"Wow, that's a gas!" Tim rubbed the soft material between his fingers.

"She won't wear it," Gena explained flatly.

"Ivy . . . Ivy . . . Ivy . . ." Tim carried the dress across the room, shaking his head slowly.

"I won't wear it, and that's that," Ivy said with finality.

"You're really a drag, Ive," Tim said sharply. She turned to face him angrily and he blurted out: "Like, how come you keep your hair like that? Seems to me, there's a better style."

Ivy's hand flew to her head involuntarily and Gena quickly handed her a compact with a mirror. No straggly ends, just dark and coarse and . . . very severe. She turned back to her work and an awkward silence filled the kitchen.

"What difference does it make?" Ivy asked finally.

"It's nothing to me," Tim said quickly, sensing at least a partial victory. "But what if you move into the city? You'll be looking to score with guys, won't you?"

Well, that made some sense, Ivy told herself reluctantly.

"Seems to me you've got to be . . . you know . . . more with the scene," he finished lamely.

"Anything else wrong with me?" Ivy asked quietly.

"I don't . . . Gena?" Tim turned to his sister for help—this was out of his line.

"Give me about twenty minutes with her," Gena said happily. "Like her lipstick. . . ."

"Yeah," Tim agreed. "It's too *red*. And maybe you should do something with her eyes."

Ivy turned to them slowly. They were talking about her as if she was . . . an *it*. As if she wasn't even there! She didn't like it. Not one little bit.

"I could do a *lot* with her eyes," Gena was saying, Tim nodding eagerly in agreement.

"Like sex them up . . . you know?" Tim's hand traced his own eye lightly.

Ivy could no longer contain herself. "You're a fine one to talk," she yelled at him. "Look at you! I agree with your father. You're a mess!"

Tim's head snapped around in surprise, speechless, his mouth half open. She knew he was hurt at her outburst, but she couldn't stop herself. Ivy looked away and turned back to the safety of her stove.

"Go take a shower," she ordered softly.

Traffic on the Long Island Expressway was light and the big Par-Tal truck moved along steadily in the right-hand lane, well within the speed limit. Jack was asleep, as he had been since the truck left the garage.

Jerry signalled with his blinker and swung out to pass an old, highly-polished Illinois license-plated Ford coupe driven by a prim gray-haired man. Jerry cursed silently and eased back into the right lane.

A buzzer sounded. He swung the phone out from under the dashboard. "Yeah?" He listened for a moment. "He's asleep. Okay." He hung up, reached over and firmly shook Jack until he stirred.

Jack protested the nudging, fighting to stay asleep. "Wha'?" He blinked his eyes a few times and stretched.

"Billy wants you," Jerry said tersely.

"Forget it." Jack half turned away and put his head back on the seat.

"He *called*," Jerry said.

"All right!"

Jack slowly stretched and began to move. He rotated his head a few times to get rid of a pressure on his neck and unzipped his coveralls. Climbing over the back of the cab seat, forced into a half crouch, he awkwardly removed the work garb and dropped it back in the cab.

Jack reached out to press a button, waited for the panel to open and stepped through. He smoothed down his carefully-tailored dinner jacket as the panel closed behind him and clicked into place.

The walls, ceiling and floor of the gambling casino on Par-Tal wheels were carpeted with heavy, deep-pile red broadloom, and the same red was repeated in the cummerbunds of the Negro croupiers and dealers. They were all young men, very attractive, very dark and uniformly dressed in elegantly-cut dinner jackets. The two beautiful waitresses, Edna and Norma, also Negro, wore short cocktail uniforms and red bows in their hair.

Billy Talbot, the other half of Par-Tal, sitting in the high chair against the back wall, overseeing the action, motioned to him.

The tables were filled to capacity and Jack walked slowly through the truck, listening to the sounds of gambling, nodding to the dealers.

"Play the field, gentlemen. . . ."

"Let's go *eleven!*"

"Blackjack for Mrs. Conklin. . . ." Mrs. Conklin, a slim woman in her late forties with a fortune in diamonds around her neck, pulled in her chips greedily, stashing them with the rest of her pile in the safety of her crooked left arm.

He passed a craps table, walked around the *chemin-de-fer* game and eased by the other twenty-one setups. He paused briefly to watch the action at Harry's dice table.

"Six is the point . . . press the nine, Mr. Franklyn? . . . who wants a field number? . . . still your dice . . ." The roller threw a seven and snarled in disgust.

Jack stopped at the small bar, snaked out an arm and caught Edna around the waist. "Bring me a coffee, will you, doll? Hot and black." She drew nearer momentarily, lips slightly pursed, and he gave her a playful shove as he continued on to the back.

Billy was wearing an elaborate lace-front shirt and an exquisitely-tied droopy red tie with his dinner jacket. His handsome face wore an expression of concern and he handed a slip of paper to Jack in greeting. "Dr. Morgan. Marker for two G's."

Jack followed Billy's eyes. A middle-aged man, going to paunch around the middle, was hunched over a pair of dice, rattling them in his palms, blowing on them through clenched hands. His voice carried over the general din. "Make numbers, dice . . . make numbers!" The doctor threw the cubes and watched them roll to a stop, his lower lip caught between his teeth.

"Seven. Shooter loses," Harry intoned. "Next shooter. Place your bets, ladies and gentlemen."

Dr. Morgan looked furtively around the room and brightened when he caught Jack's eyes on him. The doctor gestured and started toward him. Jack nodded to Billy and moved to meet him.

"Rough night, doctor?" Jack smiled easily.

"I'll come back," he said, shaking his head. "My marker okay?"

Jack walked back to the table with him. "Harry, give Dr. Morgan whatever he wants." The doctor looked relieved and Jack turned to greet the other players.

"Good evening, Mr. Brill, Mrs. Brill . . ." Jack played his part with practiced ease. He watched the doctor lose three quick bets; the Brills were betting against him and both had been winning heavily.

"He's already into us for over eleven big ones from last month," Billy told him.

"What are you worried about?" Jack broke off to take his cup of coffee from Edna, his hand lingering on hers longer than necessary. He grinned at Billy's look of disapproval and sipped the coffee with relish.

"Ever hear of the Morgan family? The banks, the whole Wall Street bit?" Jack asked finally.

"He's from those Morgans?" Billy sounded surprised.

"No, he's not," Jack said firmly. "He's a hustling chiropractor from Yonkers, so don't let him get in too deep, will you, baby?"

"Me?" Billy yelped. "You!" And he sputtered wordlessly as Jack quietly turned, ignoring him, and swept his eyes over the gambling action.

The uniform was back in Ivy's closet; the mini-dress in Gena's. They had finally compromised on a plain dark dress that showed off Ivy's excellent figure. Gena's pearls were around her neck; light eye make-up and becoming shade of lipstick made a subtle but noticeable difference in her face, and Ivy grudgingly admitted to herself that it was becoming.

Gena was still fussing over her hair, softening the line, when Tim burst into Ivy's room. His hair was wet from the shower and he wore clean but ragged khakis. "Car's coming. He's here," Tim said excitedly.

Ivy hurried for a last-minute check of the dinner and Gena followed Tim to the front hallway. They surreptitiously watched the limousine pull up to a stop; Jack got out and gave Eddie his instructions. As he walked up the lighted path Tim opened the door.

"Hey, man, you're right on time," Tim said. "Wow! You're gorgeous, man." He nodded at the dinner jacket.

Jack nodded at Tim's change of clothes in return. Tim was grinning broadly.

Gena stared at him with open admiration. "We're delighted you could come, Mr. Parks."

He nodded at her silently.

Gena gestured him into the house and started back to Ivy in the kitchen. "You'll *love* Ivy's cooking," she called over her shoulder.

Jack followed Tim and found himself alone with him in the Austin living room. He sat down on the couch. Tim plopped into a facing club chair an easy distance away.

"I thought your folks'd be here," Jack said, breaking the uneasy silence.

"Suddenly couldn't make it, man. Big fire at the store."

Jack raised his eyebrows.

"Actually, it was a little fire, but it could have been big," Tim offered.

Jack shook his head as if to say he'd better come up with a better one.

"Minor smoke damage?" Tim said. "How about a drink?" He jumped up.

"I don't drink."

51

Tim sat down and shifted his body in the chair, leaning forward. "Some pot?" he asked quizzically.

"I never touch the stuff." Jack's annoyance was palpable. "Do your parents know you have pot in the house?"

"Oh, I haven't got any," Tim said airily, throwing a leg over the arm of the chair.

"Then why'd you ask me? Suppose I'd said yes?"

"Then I'd have looked around and pretended I'd just run out."

"A lunatic!" Jack said, slapping his hands on his cuffs.

"Everybody over thirty like you thinks people my age are crazy," Tim said, defending himself. "That's the generation gap."

"And when people like you think all people like me turn on, what would you call that?" The heat in Jack's voice was barely controlled.

Tim fidgeted for a moment. "Stupidity," he acknowledged.

Jack looked around the room. Impersonal, he thought. Good taste but no soul.

Gena walked quickly into the room, carrying a tray. She was fighting Ivy off. "I'll serve them. That's my job. . . ." Ivy said in despair; she stopped protesting when Jack rose, looking at her. "Good evening," he said, his earlier hostility gone, a pleasant smile on his lips.

"Have some of Ivy's delicious hors d'oeuvres. And

please sit down." Gena was positively purring. "Tim, why doesn't Mr. Parks have a drink?"

"He claims he doesn't drink."

"Maybe some coffee," Jack offered, helping himself to a deviled egg and a small linen cocktail napkin.

"There should be some ready," Ivy said.

"I'll get it," Tim yelled quickly and hurried off. Ivy stood awkwardly in the middle of the room.

"Ivy, sit *down*," Gena ordered. "Over there." She pointed to the couch.

Ivy looked timidly at Jack and edged to the couch, sitting down gingerly as far from him as she could, her back straight. Jack took an hors d'oeuvre. "These are very good," he said to Ivy.

"Thank you." She glanced at him and smiled tentatively.

"Tell me, Mr. Parks," Gena said. "What do you think of the Black Power movement?" She had taken Tim's chair.

"Not much at all," he answered truthfully.

"You don't approve of it?" Gena asked, looking for confirmation; she wasn't prepared for his answer.

"I don't *think* of it," he said.

Tim returned, carrying coffee for Jack and helped himself to a canapé. He pulled over a large ottoman and sat down next to Gena, within easy reach of the tray.

"Ivy goes to a lot of civil rights meetings, don't you, Ivy?" Gena prodded, her voice sweet.

"Once in a while. It's a place to meet people sometimes." She was uncomfortable sitting in the living room and shifted her weight.

"I was once in an elevator with Ralph Bunche," Tim offered. "He stepped on my toe."

"That can be a problem when you wear sandals," Jack observed. He glanced at Ivy.

"He said, 'Excuse me.'" Tim reached for a deviled egg. Jack sipped his coffee. Ivy sat miserably on the end of the couch.

"I've been on lots of picket lines and things," Gena said righteously. "I was even in jail last year overnight." She paused for effect. There wasn't any. "And Ivy belongs to the N-double-A-C-P, don't you, Ivy?" Gena added, trying to bring her into the conversation.

"I . . ." Ivy twisted her hands in her lap. "Excuse me, I really have to see about the dinner." She got up quickly and fled from the room. Jack followed her with his eyes; nice legs, he thought. Not bad, not bad at all.

"I'll help," Gena offered quickly and followed Ivy into the kitchen; she was already at the stove.

"Ivy, let me . . ." Gena said.

"Just because he's colored," Ivy said, whirling about to face her, "do you have to talk about colored things?"

"I don't . . ."

"And why do you make me sit there in the living

room like that?" she continued miserably. "I don't ever do that."

"We've never had anybody like Mr. Parks before," Gena explained soothingly. "He seems to like you," she added.

"He doesn't like me. He doesn't even look at me." Ivy was surprised to realize that she cared—more than she felt like admitting.

"If you'd worn the dress I brought you . . ."

"Oh, *Gena!*" Ivy exploded.

"Ivy, this is a business thing for Tim. It'll make him look good with Dad."

"Okay," Ivy said finally. "But I'm going to serve the meal the way I'm supposed to. No nonsense about that."

"Word of honor," Gena said, smiling.

"I'll clear," Gena said and picked up the dessert plates before Ivy could protest.

"I'll get more coffee." Tim followed Gena from the room.

Suddenly Jack and Ivy were alone. Jack patted his stomach and carelessly dropped his napkin on the table. "That was a real good dinner," he said to her, relaxed for the first time since he had arrived.

"Thank you. It isn't hard when you know how." She was pleased, and smiled at him. It *had* been good.

"You learn from your mamma?"

"My gramma. She brought me up." Ivy finished her

coffee. It felt very strange sitting at the dining-room table. She had never eaten there before.

"I hear you want to split from here. Why? Looks like a pretty good setup."

"Too good," Ivy said wryly. "I don't want to die here."

"You've got to die somewhere," Jack said reasonably.

"But isn't it better if you don't go ignorant and alone?" she asked him.

Her answer surprised him and he thought about it. Then he nodded and smiled softly. "Much better," he agreed.

"I want to go to school," Ivy confided, warmed by his smile. "Maybe learn to be a secretary. I'd like to meet people."

"Where you from?" he asked suddenly.

"Florida," Ivy told him. "You're from the West Indies, aren't you?"

"You still hear it?" He smiled easily.

"Just a little." She was suddenly glad to be sitting at the table, relaxing after dinner, talking with Jack Parks.

He finished his coffee and Ivy fiddled with her spoon.

"That's a pretty shirt you've got on," Ivy said.

He glanced down.

"It was a present."

"From a girl?" she asked.

Jack nodded.

"What does she do to afford giving presents like that?" It looked very expensive.

Jack thought a minute. "She's . . . a model," he said finally, unable to recall who had given it to him.

Ivy thought it over for a minute, her face serious. "Well, I still want to be a secretary," she said finally. She took another look at the shirt. "It hasn't been pressed too well, though."

"It costs two dollars to do this at a hand laundry."

Ivy was surprised. "But it isn't a very good job."

Jack was still looking at the shirt when Tim came back into the room. He headed for the sideboard against the wall.

"Brandy, Jack?" he asked.

"No, thanks."

"Cigar?" Tim was opening a drawer.

"Your father will kill you," Ivy said. "Those are Cubans he smuggled from Canada." She got up to finish clearing the table; the mood had changed. It was strange that Tim, of all people, suddenly made her feel out of place.

Tim handed Jack a long cigar and kept one for himself.

"He knows I smoke them all the time," Tim said, waving away her protest with his hand.

"Huh!" she said, heading for the kitchen.

Jack and Tim lit up their cigars, Tim drawing

deeply and coughing; he walked out onto the patio off the dining room and Jack followed him.

"Very . . . good," Tim said seriously, holding the cigar awkwardly between his fingers.

"First rate," Jack agreed, grinning.

They sat on comfortably padded rattan chairs.

"How do you like her?" Tim asked.

"Okay," Jack said. "Not my type, though," he added quickly.

They fell silent as Ivy appeared in the dining room, to remove dishes from the table.

"Because she's a domestic?" Tim asked.

"The domestic *type*. You wind up married to a girl like that."

"Yeah . . . well, we don't want that, man," Tim said firmly.

They broke off again as Ivy returned to put the final cleaning touches on the dining room.

"Where do you go when you have a big date?" Tim asked suddenly. "Like if I wanted to take a chick for dinner someplace to really impress her."

"First I get dressed," Jack said.

"Yeah, but after that?" Tim said impatiently. "What's your favorite food?"

"Well . . . Japanese," Jack said finally. "There's a new place on Fifty-fourth Street. Pretty expensive, and you'd better call the day before." Jack flicked his cigar ash into the ashtray; Tim flicked his onto the floor.

58

Gena came out to the patio and set a tray with a fresh pot of coffee on the patio table. "I forgot the fruit."

"I'll get it," Tim said, giving Gena a big wink. He headed for the kitchen.

Ivy was working at the sink, loading the dishwasher, an apron tied around her waist. The bowl of fruit was on the table. He picked it up.

"Here," Tim said to her, "take this in to Jack and tell him it's okay for Monday night."

"What's okay for Monday night?"

"He wants to take you out."

Ivy stared at him. "He wants to take me out?"

"That's what he *said!*" Tim told her. "Dinner, a show . . ."

"He didn't ask *me!*"

"Because he figured Monday wasn't your regular day off, so he wanted to check with us first," he explained to her patiently. "I said it was fine, because the folks are going right to the club Monday for the golf banquet."

Ivy just looked at him, bewildered.

"You don't believe me? Ask Gena." Tim pointed to the door. "And get out there before he thinks you don't want to go."

"Why would he want to take me out?" Ivy asked. She dried her hands on the apron and left it folded neatly on the counter.

"Well, I *don't* think he's looking for a religious experience!"

He thrust the fruit bowl at her and steered her out the door to the patio. Jack and Gena were drinking fresh coffee; they looked up when Ivy and Tim entered.

"Would you like a pear?" Ivy asked, putting the bowl down.

"Yes, thank you," Jack said.

Ivy carefully quartered the pear with a fruit knife; Jack glanced at his watch. Tim poked her in the ribs and eluded her attempt to kick his shins.

"Monday night would be fine," Ivy said to Jack finally.

He looked at her quizzically.

"You did say Monday night?" she asked weakly, turning back to look at Tim.

"For the Japanese dinner, Jack," Tim prompted quickly.

"Monday night . . ." Jack said, looking at Ivy who was looking at Tim. Man, what a lousy trick, he thought.

"The folks won't be coming home for dinner, because of inventory." Gena said.

"The golf banquet." Tim corrected.

". . . the golf banquet . . ." Gena said, nodding.

"Monday night . . ." Jack repeated.

"If you didn't mean it . . ." Ivy looked very soft and vulnerable.

60

"No . . ." Jack said hastily. "No, Monday night would be just perfect."

They looked at each other and Ivy handed him the pear. "I forgot napkins." She lowered her eyes and quickly left the room, hurrying back to the kitchen.

Tim and Gena looked at Jack with obvious relief. He sat back, coolly puffing at his cigar.

"You two are really very cute. I'm beginning to like you," he said with a bit of grudging admiration in his voice.

"That's better than not liking us," Gena said happily.

"Like I said, man, we love you." Tim was grinning broadly.

Jack knocked his cigar ash into the ashtray, looking thoughtful. Suddenly he grinned. "In fact, my car should be here any minute, but what if I sent it away? Your folks aren't due back soon, are they?" His voice lost some of its cultured crispness.

"Not for a couple of hours," Tim said.

"Why?" Gena asked.

"Well, like, I was thinking . . ." Jack's words had taken on a conspiratorial tone. He leaned closer to Gena. "You're so interested in getting everybody together . . ." He looked straight into her eyes. "How about you and me swinging together, and let your brother take the maid?"

"You . . . and *me!* Swinging?" Gena gasped.

"Oh, come on, baby, you know what I'm talking

61

about," Jack said broadly. "It doesn't matter that you don't have pot in the house. I've got something much better in my pocket. I mean, if we all let go for a while, we could really have a ball, you know?" He moved his body rhythmically in an exaggerated jiving motion, finger-popping loudly at each of them.

"Wait a minute, man . . ." Tim interrupted.

Jack reached into his pocket and pulled out a small pillbox. He opened it and held it close to Gena so she could see what was inside.

"Like, what would you say those are?" he asked her.

"They . . . look like aspirin to me," Gena said weakly.

"They *look* like aspirin!" Jack said triumphantly.

Ivy returned with the napkins. Jack glanced up at her: "Could I trouble you for some water, please?"

"No trouble at all." Ivy went to get the water.

Tim was peering at the tablets in the pillbox. "They have 'B' written on them," he obsereved.

"B for *boffo*," Jack said. He lowered his voice. "Take two of these, and ten minutes later we'll all be swinging from the chandeliers . . . naked." He broke out into a broad grin. He was enjoying himself—these kids needed a lesson.

"Tim . . . he means an *orgy!*" Gena said, shocked.

"Listen, man, I don't think you quite get the idea," Tim said, a bit worried.

"Of course I do," Jack said. "I mean, that little colored girl in there is just a come-on, right?" He looked over to Gena and back to Tim. "I'm hip to what goes on in the suburbs with people like you. Wife-swapping, key parties . . . But that's nothing, man. Here's the real thing, a trip you'll never forget."

Gena and Tim stared at him, but their eyes were drawn back to the pillbox, to the white pills with the letter B on them. Neither of them could say a thing.

A sharp horn sounded from the driveway just as Ivy returned with Jack's water.

"Your car is here," Tim said eagerly, quickly getting to his feet.

Slowly Jack got up, smiling at Gena and Tim. He turned around, took the glass from Ivy, popped two of the pills into his mouth and he swallowed them down with the water.

"Just a little headache," he said to Ivy, smiling at her. "Monday night at seven. We'll meet at the restaurant. Three-ten East Fifty-fourth."

Jack headed for the hall, Ivy following him to the door. Gena and Tim stood on the patio.

"It was an awfully good dinner. Thanks," Jack said.

"You really don't have to, you know. Monday night, I mean." Ivy said.

They had reached the door and Jack turned back to look at Tim and Gena, now lurking at the dining-room door.

"I know I don't," Jack said to Ivy.

Ivy opened the front door for him. "Goodnight."

"See you," Jack said softly. He waved to Tim and Gena and left.

Ivy watched after him, then returned to the patio and began collecting the after-dinner-coffee dishes.

"You know," she said to Tim and Gena, "I really think he does like me a little."

They nodded at her dumbly, listening to the car move away, relieved when they could no longer hear it.

"Well . . ." Ivy asked mischievously, "want to help with the dishes?"

"There really aren't that many," Gena said.

Ivy laughed and headed for the kitchen, feeling happy.

"Tim?" Gena asked. "What do you think?"

"Either . . ." Tim broke off. "Either he really did have a headache and those were aspirins . . . or there's going to be some awful carryings-on in that car."

Chapter Five

She enjoyed the bus ride into the city, the quick changes, the disappearance of the well-kept estates, the uniformity of the rows of houses that lined the expressway, the remnants of the World's Fair, tho big apartment complexes, the neon signs and colored factory smoke, the bright white of the Queens-Midtown Tunnel, the bustle of the terminal.

Ivy decided to walk from the bus station, because she was very early; she liked New York at night—the lights, the noise, the people. She headed for Fifth Avenue and walked slowly uptown, looking in the store windows, stopping for all red lights.

She turned into Fifty-fourth Street, past exclusive

boutiques and antique galleries, the canopied ele-
gance of Sardi's East and Chateaubriand.

Gena had helped her get ready, arriving unexpectedly from the store with a beautiful, simple gold pin
for her dress and a pair of reasonable false eyelashes
that felt funny pasted to her eyelids. But they did
look nice; she hoped they would stay on all night. Ivy
looked at her reflection in a drugstore window before
crossing Third Avenue, pleased with herself, with the
hair which Gena had fussed into a soft, becoming
crown.

She crossed Third Avenue with the light, checking
the address numbers, suddenly feeling cold in the
warm night air.

Three-ten he had said, she was certain. But
three-ten was a brownstone, a house. Ivy started to
leave, stopped, then gathering up her courage she
hesitantly approached the door and tried the knob—it
was locked. A strong feeling of disappointment and
anger welled up in her, and she pulled her hand
quickly away just as the door opened and a beautiful
Japanese girl in full Geisha dress opened the door.

"Miss Moore?" she asked in a delicate voice.

Ivy nodded.

"Mr. Parks is awaiting you. Please." She gestured
for Ivy to enter and closed and locked the door behind her.

They entered the dimly-lit foyer and the girl led
the way through a noisy beaded curtain into a much

larger room behind the entranceway. The lights were dim. Four or five other Geishas were moving about, but there were no tables; the walls were lined with exquisite prints, simply framed. Along both sides of the room were small, private alcoves, each for two or more, curtained off from the rest of the room.

The hostess led Ivy to an alcove, and when they entered she found Jack already sitting on cushions next to a low table which held a lit hibachi and an assortment of foods ready to be cooked. The Geisha joined the stunningly beautiful and delicate Japanese girl who was pouring a colorless liquid into Jack's small cup.

"Hello," Jack said warmly. He did not get up.

"Some wild place," Ivy said. Tapestries covered the walls, and the little room was bathed in the warm glow of candlelight.

Jack motioned for her to sit opposite him across the narrow table. Ivy sat down awkwardly. One of the Japanese girls began to cook the first course of the dinner, working gracefully and efficiently at the hibachi.

Jack talked to the other girl in Japanese.

"I've ordered your saki warm," he explained.

Ivy watched her prepare the saki, the porcelain pitcher dully white and delicate in the warming pan.

"Doesn't she speak English?" Ivy asked.

"I guess so," he said.

"Then why did you talk to her in Japanese?"

Jack looked a little startled for a moment, then he grinned. "Maybe because I'm pretentious."

"No," Ivy said emphatically. "I'd say if you're lucky enough to know a foreign language you should practice it as much as you can. How'd you learn Japanese?"

"The army." Jack looked at her closely, noting the dress, the pin; he was pleased at the obvious change in her.

Ivy accepted the saki bowl the Geisha handed her and sipped from it delicately. She liked the warm wine. She watched the girls, intrigued with them and the place and the strange cooking, and how one of them picked up a delicate morsel from the hibachi with a pair of tiny chopsticks and offered it to Jack, and how, just as daintily, he took it in his mouth.

"Don't mind me being served first. It's an old Japanese custom," Jack explained. He sat comfortably on the cushions, at ease, his arms resting lightly on his knees, relaxed.

The second girl offered an hors d'oeuvre to Ivy. She liked it very much and said so; Jack accepted another tidbit, not moving, waiting for the girl to raise it to his mouth.

"You really like this kind of service, don't you?"

"When you're born to it, baby, you get used to it," he said offhandedly.

"Why do you pretend you haven't earned what you've got?" she asked, genuinely puzzled.

"Do I do that?" He was surprised.

Ivy nodded. "I'd think you'd be proud."

"Maybe," he said after a brief pause.

"But look at all you've done," Ivy said.

Jack lowered his gaze. The Geisha offered him another delicate morsel.

"What more do you want?" Ivy asked.

"Well, I don't want to get married," he snapped.

"Did I say you did?"

"I just want that established," Jack said firmly. He softened a bit, "I *was* married. Bad scene. Not my game."

"Well, I don't want to get married either. . . ."

"Uh-huh . . ." Jack interrupted with scorn.

"I *don't*," Ivy said indignantly. "I've scuffled for myself since I was twelve, and I'm not giving that up for some two-bit hustler." Her voice sounded harsh in the small room.

Jack looked startled.

"I don't mean you," Ivy said hastily. "What could you want from me?" It was less a question than a confession of doubt, and Ivy fell silent, shifting her weight on the cushions, suddenly uncomfortable.

The girls served at a leisurely pace, alternating between them and sharing the cooking and serving equally. Jack was enjoying the food although Ivy seemed less at ease now, and he knew she was waiting for him to speak. He surreptitiously looked at his watch and was a bit embarrassed when he realized Ivy had seen him.

"What is it you'd be giving up?" he asked her, finally.

Ivy searched for the words. "I don't know. . . ." She was quiet for a minute, and for the first time refused a bit of food the Geisha offered her. "The . . . the right to go where I want and do what I want," she said finally.

"But you've been in the same job nine years," Jack said.

"Because I've wanted to. But no more. So I'm leaving . . . no matter what they do."

Jack didn't have an answer for that, so he sat silent for a minute, glancing at his watch again. *I'm* what they're doing, he thought. And she doesn't know it.

"Why'd you come out with me if there's nothing in it for you?" he asked her.

"I didn't say that," Ivy said, and she tried to explain. "I'll have a good interesting evening. I'll steal an ashtray for my room, and that'll always remind me of what a nice dinner we had. It doesn't matter that we'll never see each other again. That happens."

She paused. Jack watched her impassively. "Anyway," Ivy continued, "we made a good trade. I get a nice dinner, and Par-Tal Trucking stays in good with the Austins."

"You do make me sound like a hustler," he was feeling uncomfortable.

"I don't mean to," Ivy said.

"Does it happen much to you?" he asked. "Guys taking you out, never calling again?"

"Once in a while," Ivy answered honestly. "But those are the dues you pay for being free, aren't they?"

He watched her silently for a moment, nodded, then looked openly at his watch.

"Look," Ivy said, "I know you've got some place else to go. I'll see a movie, then catch a late bus."

"Not a chance," Jack said, grinning. "We've got things to do, baby. You just grab that ashtray . . . and hang on."

They caught a cab at the corner, and Jack gave the driver a Greenwich Village address. They relaxed against the seat, talking easily, comfortably, full of good food. Ivy asked him about Par-Tal, and Jack told her about how he and Billy had started the trucking company and about Billy and their friendship and about their tour of duty in Japan. Ivy listened intently; she was content.

The cab let them off at the corner, to avoid backed up traffic, and they walked the half block to their destination.

It was an elaborate establishment, gaily colored with bright paint and flashing rear-projection lights: one entrance led to a theater, the other two to a jazz club and the restaurant. A line of people waiting to get into the theater stretched around the block. It was the usual Village mixture: love-beaded and flower-decked hippies; couples in evening clothes; several thin young men and women wearing bluejeans and paint-smeared work shirts; an assortment of uptown media people.

Jack put his arm firmly around Ivy's waist and steered her through the crowd and into the lobby. He walked directly to the box office and collected their reserved tickets from a bushy-haired young man in a karate suit. A uniformed policeman was standing by the door, his arms folded around his nightstick, watching the crowd of people with obvious distaste.

In the middle of the lobby, midway between the sidewalk and the entrance door, a large easel held a glass-fronted case:

NEW YORK'S LATEST SENSATION
On Stage   On Stage
SEE A LIVING FAMILY LIVE
REAL PEOPLE DOING REAL THINGS
Theater of Essence — Theater of Life

There was also a *Life* Magazine cover, blown up to triple size, showing the "Family." The Village Voice review was printed in its entirety, with the whole second paragraph underlined in red.

Another sheet of paper had review excerpts:

The New York Times: An innovation . . . interesting . . . might cause a re-examination of one's life-style. . . .

"The *Daily News:* . . . strange and baffling . . .

Time Magazine: . . . where everyone who goes anywhere is going . . .

Edwin Newman, *NBC News:* A new point in the conception of what theater is or should be.

The New York *Post:* . . . the wildest . . . a constantly changing atmosphere . . . the audience is definitely involved . . .

From the brightly-lighted lobby Jack steered Ivy through the entrance door where a young woman sitting on a high wooden stool took their tickets and motioned them through two heavy black curtains which blocked the light and dulled the sounds of the crowd milling around outside.

Ivy gasped involuntarily when she stepped through the curtains into the psychedelic world which now surrounded them. They were at the top of a flight of stairs which led down through a narrow corridor to a bright-cerise bottom landing. The black walls and the steps themselves were painted with beautifully executed oriental and astrological designs which glowed luminously in the soft light, sparkling in sequences with the rhythm of the variously-blinking lights.

Jack started down the steps, grinning with delight

at the look of wonder on Ivy's face. She stopped several times on the way down to look around, behind at the stairs they had passed, above to the color on the walls.

"It's done with infra-red light," Jack explained. He laughed. "Also known as black light."

At the bottom of the stairs the passageway turned at a right angle for a few feet and then turned again. They were in a strange, octagonal room with the corridor forming two of the sides. Just to the right of the far corridor, flat against the wall, a man was standing on his head, motionless, in a classic yoga position. Ivy was so entranced by him that at first she failed to notice the small alcove behind them and to their left, formed by two sides of the octagon which extended farther back than the others: a young man, in a dirty court-jester's costume, was balancing on a unicycle and juggling three golden balls, a cigarette dangling from the side of his mouth. He didn't look at them, and neither did the yogi when they passed him.

The corridor was dark now, and as they turned a corner it became almost pitch black. Jack took Ivy's arm to guide her, but they had only taken a step or two when a black shade flew up to their right, causing Ivy to jump against Jack with an audible gasp: a near-naked girl, spattered and smeared with streaks and spots of brightly-colored paints stared impassively at them, her eyes half open in an attempt to look interested. She was lying in a seductive pose on a platform recessed into the wall. To one side was a little table with spray-cans and a sign which read: *Paint Me.* A glass of beer, gone flat, was wedged into one corner.

Ivy stared with her mouth open, recovering from her surprise, Jack's arm was around her protectively. Solemnly, Jack walked with her closer to the girl. Disengaging his arm, he picked up one of the cans, shook it, and, with a little bow, he handed it to Ivy.

"You're supposed to paint her," he said.

"I . . . I don't think I want to."

"Okay . . ." He turned back. "Sorry," he said to the girl, and putting his arm back around Ivy's waist they continued down the corridor.

The painted girl opened her eyes and, putting her hands on her hips, she protested. "But you're *supposed to!*" she said indignantly.

Jack looked back apologetically, shrugged his shoulders, and held open for Ivy the double doors that led to the main activity.

He glanced back in time to see the corridor return to blackness as the painted girl pulled down her shade.

Ivy and Jack entered a very large room. There was a stage directly in front of a large audience, as varied in appearance and dress as the people who had been waiting on the street. Some seemed to be watching the stage intently, but others were eating and drinking; Ivy thought she even saw some people sleeping.

To their right was a small clearing, a dance floor area, bathed in its own special soft light. Sitting cross-legged in the middle of it—surrounded by a small group of people who were sitting or lying on the floor—was a trio playing Indian music: an ascetic white-robed Indian playing a sitar, a younger Indian, also white-robed, playing the tambura, and a long-haired hippie with a fluorescent orange mustache playing a fluorescent green flute.

Jack guided Ivy to their seats; he settled back, watching the stage but even more interested in Ivy's reaction. She pulled forward in her seat and looked at the stage intently. Shabby furniture, unattractive to an extreme, indicated that the actors were in a living room.

A young man in his early twenties, on a platform at the rear of the stage, his eyes reddish and slightly protruding, was drawing erratically on a sketch pad, his body moving slowly to the Indian music that hypnotically filled the room. A spotlight was shining on him, and also on a dressmaker's form that he stared at when he stopped drawing.

A man in his forties, sitting in a stained armchair placed with its side to the audience, was reading a newspaper. A woman about the same age was sitting in the center of the stage working: a bushel basket of peeled potatoes overflowed onto the stage and a huge pile of peelings lay about her feet; she finished a potato, tossed it on the floor and methodically chose from another bushel basket the next one to be peeled, discarding several before she made her choice.

A pretty, pale woman, in her early twenties like the boy, was lying immobile on an overstuffed couch which was dripping padding onto the floor from a rip in its fabric bottom. Her long, dark hair, thick and glossy in the overhead spot, flowed over the front of a long nightgown which was dingy white and looked as if it had been made from a sheet.

A man in his late twenties or early thirties sat in the right rear corner of the stage on top of three steps that led nowhere. He was holding a well-dented trumpet, and occasionally he raised it slowly to his mouth and blew a cracked note or two that sounded like an irate sports fan's razzing horn.

No one on the stage said a word or even looked at anyone else; an electrician working the lights set up on a platform over and behind the stage, visible in the glare from an improperly shielded spot, yawned. The sound was audible to the audience, but the people on stage seemed unaware of it.

"What are they *doing?*" Ivy whispered finally. She sat back in her seat and turned to face Jack.

"You can talk out loud," he said in a normal voice.

"But what's it supposed to be—a play?" Ivy whispered.

"No, they live here," Jack explained. "It's been going on for seven months. Haven't you read about it?"

Ivy shook her head. "I mostly watch TV. Old movies."

Suddenly the girl on the couch sat up and announced in a loud, clear voice, "I have to go to the john." She walked offstage past the others who continued doing what they had been doing without looking up.

Many of the people in the audience roared with laughter as the girl got up; a man sleeping in the row in front of Jack and Ivy jolted awake at the noise and instantly began applauding; part of the audience joined in. The trio stopped their *raga* and a number of the music listeners pressed down the aisles toward the stage from the rear of the room.

"What *happened!*" Ivy said, no longer whispering.

"No one *ever* says anything. They're very alienated, you see. . . ." Jack was amused at this turn of events. "Anyway," he continued, "we're very lucky to be here when someone said something."

"Huh . . . just like home. Except if I worked for these people I'd keep the place a lot neater."

Jack grinned, and taking both her hands in his, he pulled Ivy to her feet.

Chapter Six

The dour cop was gone and the waiting crowd had become reduced to manageable size when they returned past the magic black-light stairs and pushed out to the street. A soft night breeze had cleared the air and above the brightness of the Village lights was a New York rarity: a star-filled sky, the view unhindered by smoke and haze.

They walked slowly along Village streets, people-watching, enjoying themselves. An old woman with sparse, stringy gray hair, leaning out a third floor window, shrieked in Italian at the noise of a small group of young long-haired musicians holding an impromptu session in the street beneath her window. On an impulse Jack took the bongos from the boy kneeling against the wall and joined in; Ivy sat on the stoop of the building, catching the rhythm of the drums in a sway, watching him. A police car turned the corner and the group split up, slowly moving away, the old woman slamming the window in relief.

They fell into an easy conversation, the light exchange of thoughts and undirected flow of comment that comes naturally with shared pleasure—and on an impulse Ivy reached out and took his arm.

"Hungry?" he asked.

"A little bit."

He bought them knishes in a delicatessen filled with good smells and the clatter of people eating from a counter under a sign reading: *Send A Salami To Your Boy In The Army.* He handed a knish, wrapped in a napkin, to Ivy. She looked at it curiously and incautiously took a healthy bite: it was hot, and she pulled air into her mouth quickly, looking at Jack for help.

"Serves you right," he said. "There ain't *nothing* in this world don't bite back *sometime*." His eyes were laughing. "East Indian proverb," he said solemnly.

Arms linked, they stopped at a gallery window and slowly ate their knishes, watching the artist-in-residence painting with oils on the canvas propped on his easel, bringing life to the eyes of a haughty, matronly woman wearing a sable thrown over her shoulders. Ivy fought down an impulse to make a face at her, to bring her hands to her ears and wiggle them. She felt a lightness in herself—a pleasure at being alive, the new taste in her mouth a thing to be savored, the presence of Jack's arm warm and pleasantly sensual against her skin. They passed bars and pizza joints and a shop selling leather goods. A street barker hawked at customers for the strippers inside.

They passed a gaggle of noisy Texans wearing cowboy hats and making rude, drunken comments on the hippies walking barefoot on the pavement; a sidewalk cafe where a panhandler was entrancing a young couple with the story of his life; a Citröen—fully decorated with brightly-colored designs over a base of white paint, the driver's door a delight of beautifully executed minarets and paisley designs delicately intertwined, the front hood a mass of heavy, flowing swirls—idling, driverless, next to a fire hydrant.

"Voici!" A homesick graduate student jaywalked to the girl in the car. "What pleasure, the Citröen!" His accent was heavy, his eyes bore beneath the surface. "It is first I see in three months!"

They passed jewelry stores and coffee houses and tossed through a pile of psychedelic posters in a small shop filled with the sounds of acid-rock and the sweet smell of incense. Near one wall was a long counter filled with an assortment of imaginative pipes, stacks of cigarette papers and neat velvet-lined trays and rings and pins. Ropes of necklaces hung from hooks on thin wires dangling from the ceiling and Jack selected a string of delicate beads to put gently around

81

her neck and bought her two small Hindu cymbals for her fingers.

They left when a noisy trio of teeny-boppers descended the stairs into the shop.

He glanced at his watch. "It's getting late."

"Okay." She shifted the weight of the small ashtray in her purse to her other hand.

Jack checked the address on the parking lot receipt Eddie had left at the box office and they headed off. A crowd was gathered in the middle of the block around the open front of a small stall with sides of red-and-white-striped canvas which ran back from the street; sawdust from the floor spilled out onto the sidewalk. A pale, blotchy-faced young man with long bushy red hair and an unshaped beard and mustache was painting a colorful tattoo on the face of a plump, badly-dressed girl with a sallow complexion and teased platinum-frosted hair. She looked in the mirror he handed her, smiled self-consciously and left. They watched him work on a mini-skirted teenager with a Twiggy haircut, painted eyes and huge earrings; on a hippie girl from whom he refused payment; on a smartly-dressed woman Ivy thought she had once seen with Mrs. Austin at the store.

"How about it? Are you game?" Jack asked.

The brush felt funny, a soft moist pressure against her cheek, and when it was finished Ivy was delighted with the small bursting flower the mirror reflected from her cheekbone—and sorry that she would soon have to wipe it away.

She stopped to read the menu in the window of a Spanish restaurant on the corner, but Jack seemed impatient, looking at his watch again, and they walked more quickly now, talking about the foods they liked. They detoured around a barefooted girl who carried a baby in a canvas seat on her back and who was strolling with a sweat-banded, hair-in-a-bun hippie loaded down with bells that rang dully as he moved. Ivy clicked her cymbals at the boy in response. Jack laughed, and he laughed again at Ivy's momentary embarrassment. Then she clicked the cymbals in his face and took his arm and he held her tightly to his side.

The jam of people thinned to a trickle as they left the heart of the Village, and the reduction of the noise level made for a sudden, physical awareness. The normal sounds of the night and the traffic slowly took over.

Jack pointed out his car, conveniently next to the exit, unblocked, and went to pay the attendant. Ivy opened her purse on the front hood and slowly put away the beads from her neck and the finger cymbals.

Jack watched silently through the window of the booth.

"Look, I could run you out home," Jack said.

"I really prefer the bus, thanks."

They were riding up an escalator in the West Side Bus Terminal, standing stiffly in the harsh glare of the unremitting lights, the only people in sight. Their voices sounded strange in the anonymous space.

"How about letting me buy you a cab? Last of the big spenders, you know?" His attempt at lightness fell flatly around them.

"No, honest." Her voice said that it was final.

"Actually . . . there's still time for me to do some work," he said truthfully.

Ivy glanced over at him. "No wonder you're so successful, working nights."

"It hasn't been easy." Jack meant it . . . and he felt uneasy. She hadn't been sarcastic—she'd meant what she'd said and no more. He had an awful feeling that he was going to feel guilty about this; sarcasm would have made it easier. Much easier, he thought wryly.

They got off the escalator directly onto a departure platform. A soldier, curled on one side around his duffle bag, was asleep on a bench, and two nattily-dressed college boys talked animatedly with a girl on another. The platform had the dismal, empty look of late night; a porter at the far end was slowly mopping his way toward them.

"Lucky. You've only got six minutes to wait for the one o'clock," Jack said. They walked along the platform, chose a bench and Ivy sat down.

"I'll wait for the three thirty," she said.

"Why?" Jack asked.

"If I get home too early, I'll never be able to con-vince Tim and Gena that I had a wonderful time," she said honestly.

Jack stood looking into her upraised face. "So you're going to sit here for two and a half hours?" He didn't want to believe her—she had to be kidding!

Ivy nodded,

"Girl, that's crazy!"

She opened her purse and pulled out a paperback, the cymbals clinking lightly. "I came prepared," Ivy said simply.

Jack shook his head and whistled softly. "I'd take you up to Small's for a couple of hours. Or maybe up to my place."

"But I have to work," he said quickly, fighting himself. Damn it, I really *am* going to work, thanks to Billy.

"Well," Ivy smiled at him, "I've had a wonderful time."

"Yeah," Jack agreed. "Well, goodnight."

"Goodnight."

Jack stopped at the top of the down escalator and looked back. She had wet the corner of a handker-chief at her mouth and was removing the tattoo with the aid of a small mirror. He took a *Times* and a *News* from their vending machines and walked the papers back to her.

"Here."

"Thank you. I was going to get them when you left."

He turned to go, then stopped again. "You should have left that on," he said, pointing to her cheek. "It looked very pretty. Doesn't matter what people think."

Ivy couldn't answer.

"See you."

The one o'clock bus pulled up to the loading platform; the soldier bolted awake. At the top of the escalator Jack looked back a last time: by herself on the bench, half the platform distance away from anyone else, slowly turning a page of the *News*, Ivy looked very small, very alone.

He quickly walked down the moving escalator.

Tim was pacing, a cigarette in one hand, an empty can of beer in the other, his bare feet picking their way across the cluttered floor. Dylan whined softly from the one functioning channel of the stereo. Earlier he had wrapped himself in the sheets on the couch in an attempt to sleep, his eyes opening at the sound of each building drone and fading out as cars passed at growing intervals on the main road.

Now he tossed the empty can in a corner and took the last beer from the bathroom sink, discarding the aluminum pull-tab in the tub. From the window he could see a light in Gena's room across the lawn in the main house. Ivy still wasn't home.

He switched on the bulb and studied his face in the mirror, pushing the hair back off his forehead. He touched his upper lip. Yeah . . . a droopy one to the corners of the mouth. Or maybe curling up and finger-twisted at the ends?

The needle clicked rhythmically against the stop groove of the record. Tim tossed it aside and chose another at random. He made a mental note to have the faulty speaker repaired. He was as nervous as the proverbial father-of-the-bride.

"If she really leaves, I've had it," Tim said aloud. The sound of his voice hung in the air for a long time.

"And *then* what happened?" Gena pulled her chair closer.

"Well, and then there was this weirdy family living on a stage."

"Does the runaway priest still hang out with them?" Tim wanted to know.

"The one with the trumpet?"

"That's him," He nodded vigorously; the top of his scruffy terrycloth robe opened. "Two weeks ago in the *Voice* it told how he almost scored with the mother."

"And then what happened?" Gena asked, glaring at Tim to be quiet.

They were sitting at the breakfast table, drinking coffee, spotlighted by the round fixture overhead, the smoke from Tim's cigarette suspended in the light.

Ivy told them everything she could remember, stretching it out to please them, wanting to go to bed. Tim interrupted frequently with endless comments, quoting the *Village Voice*, repeating stories from his friends and about them and showing off his knowledge of what *really* was happening. Gena, wearing an elaborate and very seductive negligee, finally kicked his shin in disgust. Ivy showed them the necklace and cymbals.

"And then what happened?" Gena asked.

Through the window Ivy saw that the sky had lightened with the first pink touch of dawn. She poured another cup of coffee. And she hoped she could tell them what they were waiting to hear.

"Well . . ." she said finally.

Gena and Tim looked at her expectantly.

"Well . . ." Ivy continued, taking a deep breath, "then we went uptown to Small's and danced for a couple of hours, and . . . then we were hungry again . . ." She fingered the beads.

"Uh-huh!" Gena grinned triumphantly. "'Come up to my pad, baby, for some scrambled eggs,'" she mimicked broadly, dropping her voice an octave and squaring her shoulders.

Tim snorted a high laugh.

"No," Ivy said firmly. "We had something to eat downstairs at Small's."

Ivy waited for the disappointment to register on her face. "*Later* we went to his place."

Gena laughed appreciatively. "What kind of place does he have?"

"Where is it?" Tim asked, annoyed as he felt a pang of jealousy. What a self-inflicted complication, he thought. He was almost successful in ignoring it.

"It's . . . you know, somewhere uptown," Ivy answered. That's safe, she thought.

"A nice apartment?" Gena asked.

"The usual bachelor place." She broke off, drinking coffee, and created Jack's apartment in her mind. "Oriental stuff from when he was in Japan. A brand-new kitchen. Lots of books and records and a color TV," she said firmly and without hesitation.

"Bet it could use your touch," Gena said.

Ivy shook her head. "He has a woman come in to clean every day."

Gena raised her eyebrows.

"An *older* woman."

"Are you going to see him again?" Tim toyed with his cup, swirling the coffee around until it splashed out on his saucer.

Ivy got up quickly and picked up their cups and saucers from the table. "Hey," she said, "it's six o'clock."

"We'll do that!" Gena took the dishes from Ivy to the sink. "What's his bedroom like?" she asked casually.

"None of your business!" Ivy drew the line fiercely. Gena dawdled at the sink until Ivy pushed her away. "Do you realize I have to be up in two hours to make breakfast?"

"Mom said you don't have to bother," Gena told her.

"They didn't even expect you back before like noon," Tim added.

Gena cleared the table, her white satin mules slapping loudly on the floor. Ivy rinsed the last cup and dried her hands on a towel. "It's not my day off," she said to them. "I'll make their breakfast like I always do. Yours, too. Now get to bed."

"Okay." Gena didn't move.

Tim stopped Ivy at the door to her room. "Did he or didn't he ask for another date?"

Ivy paused. "He said he'd call," she told him. "Now, goodnight!" She shut him out of her room.

Tim looked morosely at his sister.

"Nothing," he said.

"Really nothing," Gena agreed.

"He didn't even ask her out again." Tim ran a hand through his hair, pushing it off his forehead.

"Well . . . that's the end of that." She waved goodnight and went upstairs.

Tim looked at his feet thoughtfully and lit a cigarette. He crumpled the empty pack and threw it on the counter.

Chapter Seven

The gambling truck, in the middle of a three-truck Par-Tal convoy, was rolling along in the right-hand lane of a New York State highway well-traveled by trucks at night. They were moving at a steady five miles below the speed limit, carefully obeying traffic regulations.

Jerry was driving, humming softly under his breath as usual, even though Jack was awake for a change. Jack waved off Jerry's automatic move for the buzzing phone and answered it himself.

"Yeah, Billy. . . . He is? I didn't see him get aboard." Jack frowned, smelling trouble.

Billy was in his usual spot, on the high stool in the rear corner of the gambling truck, overseeing the action and maintaining contact with the cab through the phone in his hand. "He ran in the last second," he told Jack, "and he keeps asking for you."

Billy looked over at a blackjack table in the middle of the truck. Tim, making a concession, had put on a sport jacket and even a tie, although he wore a pair of old khakis and his sandals. Even dressed properly he would stand out like a sore thumb, Billy thought. An impressive number of chips were stacked in front of Tim and he had just received an ace as his up card.

"How do I know what he wants?" he asked Jack. "*You* deal with him, man!" Billy hung up the phone in disgust.

Tim had flipped up his hole card. "What do you know—my first blackjack," he said brightly. The dealer completed the round, drew a card and went over. Tim drew in his chips and glanced over.

Billy nodded to let him know Jack was on the way and watched, annoyed, as Tim won the next three rounds with pat hands. Billy fantasized himself breaking the kid with a marked deck and quickly shook his head, looking away. It was too damn tempting. He signalled the waitress to put on coffee for Jack and he lit one of his infrequent cigarettes. There was going to be trouble, he knew it. The sweet way he'd roped Jack into that date—yes, sir, this sure was no kid to have around!

Tim moved his chips to Harry's craps table at the

front of the truck. Billy moved off his stool and called the extra dealer over to fill the chair, then wended his way forward.

"Twenty on the come, Harry," Tim bet.

"Lay it down, man." Harry pointed.

Billy watched Tim drop chips on the come line; Jack entered from the panel, smoothing down his jacket. He signalled Billy to be ready . . . in case.

Jack waited for Tim to throw the dice. "You looking for me?"

"A two and a one . . . craps . . . collect from the line," Harry intoned and pushed the dice back to Tim.

Tim glanced over at Billy and then at Jack. "Pass new dice," he said to Harry, tossing the pair in his hand. Harry looked for Jack's nod of okay, then passed a new pair to the next shooter.

"Buy me a drink," Tim said, pocketing the dice.

"Sure."

They threaded their way the length of the truck, Tim in the lead, to the rear near Billy's perch. Jack's coffee was poured, waiting for him, and he nodded his thanks to the waitress behind the bar.

"I'll have a brandy," Tim said.

She poured the drink and left immediately at Jack's signal. Billy motioned the relief man down and climbed back on the stool himself, keeping a careful eye on the bar.

"What's on your mind, man?" Jack asked.

"When are you going to call Ivy again?"

"Go away, boy!" Jack's voice was soft but there was no mistaking him.

"Don't blow your cool, man." Tim raised his hands in the age-old gesture of misunderstood politicians.

"I'm not blowing my cool!" Jack said, raising his voice. He talked rapidly. "When I blow my cool, you get washed. Clear? Now she's been your family's maid. She doesn't want to be your family's maid anymore. She wants to split." Jack leaned close to him and drew out his words: *"That's all there is to it!"*

"Wrong, man." Tim shook his head vigorously. "I was a kid when Ivy came. She's been with us almost half my life. She's more like a sister."

"Well, I don't want to marry your sister!" Jack said angrily. Billy signalled the relief man again and quickly walked to the bar.

Tim toyed with his glass. "I just want you to take her out again."

"You take her out!"

"I've thought of it, I've thought of it," Tim said seriously. "When I was seventeen, we were alone one night watching TV, and I made a move. She laughed at me, and I sprained my ankle." He looked at Jack and grinned sheepishly. "And don't think *that* didn't come up in my analysis. I can't bear rejection."

Billy stationed himself behind the bar. "Something wrong, Jack?" he asked, looking straight at Tim.

"Hippy-dippy here is out of line."

"Lay off, man," Billy said. "He did his duty."

Tim held out his glass and pointed for a refill. "You married, Billy?"

"Separated."

Tim looked over at Jack and back again. "Maybe you two could alternate," he suggested seriously.

Billy leaned on the bar and tapped Jack on the shoulder. "We're circling New Rochelle," he said. "Could we drop him off at a lonely cemetery?"

"Dead or alive?" Tim asked, cheerfully unconcerned.

"It's your choice, man," Billy said, turning back to him, tightening his grip on the bottle of brandy.

Tim drummed his fingers slowly on the bar and sipped his drink, smiling pensively. "I could make you," he said to Jack, softly.

"Go home and play with your daddy's money, sonny boy."

Tim pursed his lips, brushed his hair back from his forehead and slowly extracted the dice from his pocket. He held them up and slowly turned the bar stool so he faced the gambling, his back to the bar.

"I could make a loud, indignant announcement that these are loaded," he said slowly, drawing out the words.

Billy stared at the back of Tim's head, horrified; Jack grabbed out quickly for his arm. "You're going to get smashed!" he hissed.

"I would," Tim said firmly.

"Into little pieces," Billy snarled.

Tim opened his mouth to make the announcement and Jack's left hand shot out to gag him. He easily turned Tim around, forced an arm up behind his back and quickly shoved him into the corner to avoid attention. Billy immediately positioned himself in front of them to obscure the view of the gamblers.

"Give me those dice!" Jack demanded.

Tim mumbled behind Jack's hand. "All . . . you have . . . to do is . . . take her out . . . one more time."

"No!" Jack tightened the grip on Tim's arm painfully as the boy struggled briefly to free himself; Jack kicked him on the ankle for trying to bite.

Jack glanced over his shoulder—the dealers at the near tables were pointedly ignoring them, close enough to *know* there was trouble; Harry, at the far end of the room, glanced over worriedly, unable to be sure.

A few of the gamblers were getting curious and Billy moved to block off their viewing angle.

"Better go cool them out," Jack said softly. "But get your relief here to cover first. And make some noise to cover up!"

Tim squawked audibly. Billy forced a little laugh, clasped his hands behind his back and rocked on his heels until the relief man took over, sizing up the situation for himself.

Billy decided the simplest approach was best so he

waved to distract the only persistently curious woman and headed for her table.

"Hi there, Mrs. Clark!" he said jovially, leaning over to block her view. A weasel-faced woman in her sixties, she was addicted to roulette. A pile of chips was crooked in the safety of her arm. Billy fingered them as he heard a faint squawk, raising his hand and letting them fall clinking to the table. "I see you're having a big night." She nodded happily.

"All bets, please." The wheel began to spin, drowning out the sounds from the back and as she did every third or fourth roll, Mrs. Clark placed her chip on a line in a flagrant attempt to cover two numbers with the same bet. She rarely got away with it. Now Billy signalled the croupier to let her cheat until things settled down. She won and Billy suppressed a snarl: on top of everything else, that damn kid was costing them money! The croupier pushed her winnings across the table and Billy helped her rake them in: he laughed suddenly to drown out a voice in the corner.

"I said *no!*" Jack had yelled in Tim's ear.

Chapter Eight

Ivy hung up the phone in Gena's room and slowly finished dusting, inadvertently doing the cutglass perfume bottles on the bureau a second time. She stopped at the window and silently watched the play of sunlight on Long Island Sound; a large speedboat cut a spreading swath in its wake and the water surface mended itself slowly as the whine of the motor passed.

That's the *worst* that could happen, she thought. A temporary change. But I'd still be Ivy, just like that's still Long Island Sound. There's not a reason worth its salt for not trying!

She left the room in determination, elated, pausing at the hall closet long enough to throw the dusting cloth in the rag hamper; she disposed of the waste-basket trash and headed for her room.

It took less than a minute to place the entire contents of her closet—uniforms excepted—on the bed. She stood staring at her meager wardrobe, painfully aware of its unsuitability. On an impulse she headed back upstairs.

The Austins had converted what once was Gena's playroom into a huge combination dressing room-closet that was the envy of her female friends. A professional make-up light was mounted on the wall over a vanity table, and a three-way mirror separated two tiers of shelves filled with labeled shoeboxes and handbags in plastic protectors. A cedar chest lightly scented the room.

The built-in racks were jammed with clothes and Ivy shopped through them carefully, rejecting mini-dresses and long gowns out of hand, occasionally pulling a dress off its hanger to hold against her uniform in front of the mirror. Slowly she began to narrow her choice, leaving the decision open until the very end; but there was not the slightest doubt. The blue silk was so simple. Simple but so very beautiful. I'm twenty-six years old, she thought, and I've never had a beautiful dress. She carried this one with her to the phone, dialed the store and waited for the switchboard to make the connection.

"Gena? It's Ivy."

"Hi. What's up?"

"Well . . ." Ivy blurted it out: "Listen, I should of asked and I hope you don't mind but I looked through your closet and . . ."

"Mind? Why should I mind, Ivy? You've been taking care of my clothes for years. Is there something wrong?"

"No, there's nothing wrong, it's just that . . . well . . . I'd like you to help me find a special dress."

"You've got a date!" Gena sat down next to the phone.

"Yes. Thursday night."

"Let me guess. It couldn't be that *dashing* Jack Parks by any chance?" My God, she wondered. How did Tim do it?

"Yes, it is," Ivy said happily. "He called a little while ago to ask and I want to have a new dress."

"Great!" Gena said. "We've just gotten in some terrific stuff from England and it isn't even all unpacked yet, but . . ."

"No," Ivy interrupted. "No mini-dress and nothing kooky. I know what I want. I want something like your blue silk dress. Something simple," she said firmly. "Simple but beautiful."

"Well, I certainly can't argue you out of that one," Gena admitted. "It *is* a nice dress. But I don't carry anything like that in the Boutique." Gena glanced thoughtfully over the racks near a display of pop music record jackets.

"Oh. Of course not." Ivy sat down on Gena's bed, looking at the dress.

"Tell you what," Gena suggested. "I'll look around the dress department and bring some stuff home tonight for you to try on." She slowly turned back to the display. "No, wait a minute," she said quickly. "I've got a better idea. Are you almost done with the house?"

"I'm all done," Ivy said. "Even dinner. I made a stew yesterday so it could sit overnight. Stew's always better the second day."

"Good. I'll come pick you up after lunch and bring you here. That way I can help with the accessories. See you about two. 'Bye."

Gena hung up quickly to avoid any possible protest and walked to the display. Yes, she thought. That would do nicely. *Very* nicely. She unpinned an album jacket and signalled a salesgirl to cover for her.

Austin's Beauty Shoppe was on the fourth floor, directly to the right of the elevators through a curtained glass door. It was a multi-service operation, providing a full-time make-up consultant and a by-appointment masseuse in addition to the hair stylists. Irene, the manager of the shop, had been with Austin's since the day the Shoppe opened and she prided herself on maintaining a high level of professional beauty care and on having a remarkably small turnover of her staff. They were paid good salaries and received handsome tips from well-satisfied customers who came back again and again.

Gena took her aside, "Irene, do you have any Negro customers?"

"Well, occasionally the colored girl who works in Children's Clothes comes up, and once or twice we've made a phone appointment who turned out to be colored but that's about all." Irene lowered her voice. "Frankly, I'm just as glad. The operators don't like working on their hair. It's . . . *different,*" she said lamely.

"Well, that's too bad, but I want you to do me a favor anyway. I'm bringing our maid to the store later to find a dress and then I'm bringing her up here. Giver her the works: manicure, facial, make-up hints. And most of all I want something done with her hair. It's very important to me, Irene."

Irene frowned and looked over at the girls. "Well," she said slowly. "Beatrice usually takes the colored girl from downstairs, and she does a pretty good job." They walked back to the desk and Irene checked the appointment book. "We can squeeze her in at three thirty. How's that?"

"Fine. That'll give us enough time for the dress first. Her name's Ivy Moore. And look, tell Beatrice that a pretty good job isn't good enough." Gena handed Irene the album jacket. "Tell her to cut it something like this, soft around the sides and . . . you know."

"Okay." Irene signalled for Beatrice.

Gena thought a minute. "Better make an appointment for her to have a comb-out on Thursday, too. About four o'clock."

Irene noted it in the book. "The make-up might be a problem," she said suddenly. "I think they use something special."

"Well then, find out about it! Make some phone calls. Get the name of the nearest place and send the store messenger for it. Tell your make-up girl to demonstrate on a model today if she has to—just as long as she has what she needs for Ivy by Thursday."

"Okay, okay. We'll treat her like the Queen of Sheba if that's what you want."

"No," Gena said. *"That's* not necessary. All I want is for you to make her beautiful."

Irene threw up her hands.

"Oh, and before I forget. I'll need a set myself on Thursday. Got a date with Freddy. Can you take me yourself?"

Irene nodded and marked the appointment in her book.

"Okay. *Okay* already," Jack shouted. "Lay off it!"

"Sure, man," Billy said. "Don't want no hassle, do we, Jerry?"

"No sirree! Noooo hassle," Jerry agreed, shaking his head slowly.

"Right. That's what I said. No hassle." Billy looked

103

back at Jack solemnly. "Only one small problem," he said. "You've already *had* your night off this month, buddy. How about that?"

"Now just wait a minute! Just you wait a minute," Jack yelled. You were *there*, man! He wasn't going to ruin just the *Parks* part of Par-Tall"

"Maybe not. Maybe not. But we'll never know, will we?" Billy asked sweetly. "So I *ain't* working for the both of us so you can cut out to Romeo some lonely, innocent, stuck-in-the-suburbs maid you've got the hots for!"

Jerry burst out laughing.

"Look," Jack said, barely controlling his anger. "I will *grant* you that she's not so bad looking. I might *even* go so far as to say that considering the circumstances"—he punched a finger against Billy's chest— "*considering* the circumstances, I had a surprisingly pleasant evening."

The nodded expressions Billy and Jerry exchanged would have meant "Sure, sure," to anyone, anywhere in the world.

"Now wait a minute, you guys, what I mean is she *could* have been two hundred pounds with carrot-dyed hair and a wrinkled flowered dress!"

"Sure, Jack," Jerry said, his head bobbing in exaggerated agreement.

"We *understand*." Billy leaned over close to him. "You don't have to get *upset* about it, buddy. *We* understand."

Jack stormed out of Billy's bedroom into the working office the architect had meant to be a living room. Plain metal filing cabinets rested against two walls, facing furniture that was equally functional. A good-sized map of the United States, behind glass in a plain black frame, shared the back wall with a large chart summarizing the traffic and driving laws of New York State. It was still early, and one girl was easily tending all four radiophones in the middle of the room.

Jack started around the phones, heading for the hall and his own apartment, but instead he circled, passed the desks, and stormed back into the bedroom.

"And *furthermore*," Jack yelled at them, "I have been blackmailed not once but *twice* into taking out this *nut* who waits two-and-a-half hours in the West Side Bus Terminal because she thinks if she gets home late that miserable hippie who's *blackmailing me* into taking her out will think *she's* had a wonderful time. And this you call *copping out? I* call it being crapped *on!*" Jack slammed the door viciously on his way out.

Unstoppable tears of laughter streamed from Jerry's eyes.

Ivy almost refused the offer automatically, but she stopped herself in time, the dress box clutched firmly to her side. "Why, that would be very nice, Gena. Are you sure Freddy won't mind?"

"No, of course not, silly. We're heading right for

the city Thursday night anyway and we'll put you in the first empty cab in Manhattan."

"That would be just fine."

Gena glanced over at her. Tim's not going to believe his eyes, she thought, anticipating his expression with glee. But then, who would have believed it? Irene had actually done what Gena asked: she'd made Ivy beautiful.

Beatrice had cut Ivy's hair short in back, then tapered the long hair on the crown to frame the sides of her face in soft, deceptively simple layers, bringing it forward on her forehead in carefree pixie bangs. And even though Irene had been right about the make-up—the cosmetician swore she'd have it by Thursday—the new hairstyle was enough by itself.

"I have an appointment with Irene Thursday afternoon," Gena said. "I'll tell Freddy to pick us up at the store and we can use the Boutique dressing room to get ready. That way we won't have to hurry."

"Fine," Ivy said. "That sounds just fine."

Gena helped carry the packages into her room and when she left Ivy carefully locked the door. She showered quickly, toweled dry and carefully patted on deodorant powder.

She unwrapped the silk underthings first, testing them against her skin before putting them on. Stockings attached, her toes wriggling in the new shoes, she finally decided to try stepping into the lace half-slip. And then she ripped the protective tissue paper

106

from the dress and slipped it on quickly, struggling with the zipper.

It was a lovely dress, the material incredibly soft and lightly self-patterned. It was cut respectably low in front and back, the skirt gently tapering from the tight-fitting midriff and narrow waist to end in a scalloped hem above her knees.

She took a beaded bag and gloves from their plastic cases, arranging them comfortably in one hand and slowly opened her closet door to expose the full-length mirror.

"Billy, were you joshing Jack about tonight?" Jerry asked.

They were eating breakfast at high noon in the communal dining room down the hall from Billy's apartment; Jerry had walked up the three flights from his place on the seventh floor as he did every morning, his one concession to exercise.

"Nope." Billy fished with a spoon for a piece of the hard roll he had lost, dunking, in his sweetened coffee.

Jerry thought about it for a minute. "Good," he said finally.

"Good? You're going to be stuck with him up front for at least a couple of hours. And if he's still steaming at me, you can bet he'll pass up his nap."

"Don't care," Jerry said. "And I'm sure he'll be steaming."

"How come?" Billy asked.

"Well, to put it simply," Jerry said, "Somehow I *know* that cat would've found a way out easy enough . . . if he hadn't decided, suddenlike, that it wasn't such a bad thing to be *forced* into." Jerry leaned over, his arms resting on the table. "Maybe he just doesn't want to admit to liking some homely maid. And if he won't admit it . . . he shouldn't do it. That's bad for the *soul*, man, you know that." Jerry was grinning.

Billy looked at him thoughtfully, slowly breaking out in a full, wide grin. "Jerry, my boy," he said, tapping him lightly on the back of a hand with his spoon, "You've got him pegged like a dime-store butterfly."

Chapter Nine

Ivy's cab pulled to the curb in front of a large, sol-idly-built building on the Upper West Side, off River-side Drive. Although of the same pre-war vintage as the other apartment houses nearby, its recently sand-blasted façade and polished number plate served to underline the run-down condition of the rest of the block.

The George Washington Bridge, brilliantly decked in its night lights, stood sentinel over the Hudson, majestic and looking very near; headlights on the bridge moved into Manhattan with deceptive slow-ness, a constant ribbon of flickering brightness. She wondered if Jack's apartment had the view.

The building had no doorman, but an elderly

Negro in a uniform rose from a bench near his
switchboard when Ivy entered; he came toward her
across the long lobby.

"Yes, ma'am? Can I help you?" He doffed his cap.

"Mr. Parks's apartment, please."

"Is he expecting you?" The old man was very po-
lite.

"Yes, he is."

"Tenth floor," he told her. "I'll call on ahead."

Ivy paused at the elevator. "What apartment?"

"Just the tenth floor, Miss."

Ivy shrugged, pushed the button, and the doors of
the elevator closed.

The old man rang the tenth floor. "Mighty pretty
young lady on the way up. Asking for Mr. Parks. . . .
No, I didn't ask her name."

Jerry rang for the elevator. He had dangerously extended his nap which meant rushing through his dinner to be ready on time. He fumbled with the zipper
on his coveralls, cursing as it jammed on some loose
material; he was still trying to free it when the elevator door opened. A girl was the only passenger.

He pushed ten; she stopped at the threshold, then
moved back when she saw they were on seven. Jerry
freed the zipper and glanced up. She was looking at
the indicator. Well, well, he wondered. Now who
could that belong to? If she were mine, I'd lock her
out of sight.

They reached ten and Jerry quickly headed out of sight through the door across the hall.

Ivy left the elevator, suddenly uncertain of herself. There were three other doors, she saw, and two of them were also open. There were no signs and no directory; Jack was nowhere in sight. Several men turned to look at her as she walked from one door to another, but a number of others and the few women seemed uninterested; a dog barked shrilly over the music drifting from the far door and the jumble of voices, seemingly sourceless, collected in the empty space.

Ivy moved tentatively toward the door across the hall.

Billy liked this time of day, the busyness and the sounds and looks of the radiophones in the office-née-living room; now each phone had an operator. All four of the attractive Negro girls wore the same shiny plastic dresses with a wide, gold-studded belt; their mini-dresses had a distractingly short hemline. Harry was seated at the back desk poring over a ledger and making notes on a scratch pad.

Billy worked with the girls, dictating instructions for each radiophone in rotation. He was making and confirming reservations and scheduling the night's pick-ups, carefully keeping the master book in his hand up to date.

He decided on Eddie's pick-up. "Tell him eight

forty, Eighty-seventh and Park, Willis and a party of five." Billy checked it off in the book and moved on.

"Eddie . . . eight forty. Eighty-seventh and Park, Willis and a party of five," the girl repeated into the radiophone.

"Where's Theo?" Billy asked of the girl on the end.

"Ninetieth Street and East End," she told him.

"That's good," He nodded his approval. "Tell him eight fifty, across from Gracie Mansion, Mr. and Mrs. Stanton."

The girl called into the radiophone: "Theo . . . eight fifty. Across from Gracie Mansion, Mr. and Mrs. Stanton . . ."

As Ivy neared the closer of the two doors at the end of the hall, voices became distinct and she could hear a woman—no, it's two women, she thought—repeating instructions: ". . . across from Gracie Mansion, Mr. and Mrs. Stanton. . . ."

Wrong by half, she told herself, looking at the backs of the four girls working the microphones. She looked around for Jack, disappointed when she saw he wasn't there. The man giving instructions glanced up and did a double-take at her, staring for a second and then pointed and silently mouthed "Wait," and signalled "One minute," with his hand when a phone rang. The girl on the end took it.

"I'm sorry, Mr. Shaw, but we're booked through Monday, unless you want a single tomorrow night?"

She scribbled on a piece of paper and handed it to the man; Ivy watched him check his book and nod. Were they reserving hotel rooms?

"Yes," the girl said. "We can take six on Tuesday. Fine, you're all set." She transfered the receiver to her other ear and pushed a button on the phone.

"Hello, Par-Tal," she said, stressing the "Tal" slightly.

Ivy felt a slight surge of relief—at least she was getting closer. And perhaps this man knew where to find Jack. But the excitement that had been building in her these past days—fanned by the Austins' surprized compliments the Tim's unbelieving "Ivy, you look beautiful," and bolstered by the attention, the easy teasing Gena and Freddy had kept up all the way into the city—the excitement she had felt grow even stronger these past few hours was now slowly turning sour, going flat . . . the pleasure in her new appearance fading to self-consciousness as she watched the plastic-dressed girls; she suddenly felt overdressed and old-fashioned—abandoned.

The man waved to catch her attention and signalled, "One more minute." Ivy nodded to him.

"Oh, hi, Dr. Green. . . . Alone . . . tomorrow?" The man nodded an okay. "No problem. Same place? Fine, you're set." The girl hung up the receiver and turned back to the radiophone; Ivy watched with relief as the man patted her on the head and walked toward the door.

"Hello," he said. "You just come up?"

"A few minutes ago. I'm looking for Mr. Parks's apartment."

In unison, without breaking off their work, the girls turned to look at Ivy, then at each other as if perhaps one of them could identify this stranger.

The man gently guided her into the hall for privacy's sake. "Honey, I'm sorry," he said. "But Jack's busy tonight."

And I didn't bring a book, she thought ruefully. "Oh . . . Well . . ." There really was nothing she could say. Would this stranger care that a numbness had followed his words into her head?

She turned and mechanically moved back to the elevator.

The man stopped just inside the door and turned back after her. "Hey," he called. "Shall I say you were here?"

"That's all right," she said. "It's not important."

"Please, what's your name?" he asked.

"Ivy Moore." She reached the elevator and pressed the *Down* button.

"*Wait* a minute!" he yelled, catching up and taking her arm. "He's got a date with *you*."

Ivy looked at him flatly. "I *thought* he did," she said. And suddenly she began to feel angry.

"I'm Jack's partner, Billy Talbot," he explained, looking at her slowly. "My mistake." He took her arm. "You come with me."

They walked back to the door of the room. "Harry," he called. "Take over the pick-ups." Billy handed him the book; Harry glanced at the open page, tapped a girl on the shoulder and went to work: "Mrs. Kling and two, Number One Fifth Avenue . . . give them to Eddie at eight twenty-five. Tell Perry to get Wetherell and three at U.N. Plaza at eight-thirty."

Ivy followed Billy toward the closed door at the end of the hall. "Is this the Par-Tal office?" she asked.

"The best part of it," Billy said, grinning. He opened the door and stepped back to let her enter. So this is Jack's "homely" maid, he thought. Boy, were we ever off base!

The apartment was a shock to Ivy: it was totally different, much more personal and considerably larger than she could have ever guessed—and all she could really see yet was the living room

"Jack!" Billy yelled, shutting the door behind them. Music poured out of hidden speakers throughout the spacious living room, the throbbing sound of a beautifully played electric guitar pounding out the beat for the singing group. The far wall of the room was dominated by a huge, well-stocked tropical-fish tank: a seemingly endless variety of multi-colored fish swam lazily through the water, exploring the plants and rocks of their domain. Ivy drew nearer, fascinated, but her eyes were also drawn to the collection of thoughtfully-framed children's paintings on the other full wall: many of them were large and ambitious, all

115

but the portraits of Jack relating to the apartment or the building or Par-Tal Trucking. Through open doors she could see a dining room and a den filled with books from ceiling to floor—and she was glad to discover that she hadn't been totally wrong: a half dozen Negro children, surely all below the age of eight, were sitting on the den floor watching a huge color television set. The children looked up at Billy's yell; they glanced shyly at Ivy for a moment, until the television reached out to reclaim their attention.

She looked at them shyly, too, and then watched an adventuresome fish swim through a maze of artificial coral.

Jack frowned at Billy's yell but he moved quickly, closing the bedroom door behind him and striding down the connecting hall. He was dressed casually, in slacks and a sports shirt, and he stopped short of the living room at the sight of Ivy by the fish tank, half turned away from him, engrossed as a child.

I don't believe my eyes, he thought, staring at her through the doorway. I don't *believe* it.

He slowly crossed the room to join her, ignoring Billy's impatient movements by the door.

"Evening . . ." she said, looking up at him.

Jack nodded, still staring.

"Man, it's *late*," Billy moaned, walking closer. "And you're not dressed!"

"I'm taking out Miss Moore."

"You'll take her with us," Billy said, grasping Jack's arm to turn him around.

"Billy, these twenty-hour days have got to stop!" Jack protested, his teeth clenched.

"I *need* you, man."

"But what happens when I need you in the *daytime* operation?" Jack's voice was shrill.

"Not my bag," Billy shrugged as if it was all perfectly easy and understandable.

"But this is *my bag*," Jack said sarcastically. "Somehow that doesn't make sense."

"All in how you look at it," Billy said lightly. "See you downstairs in twenty minutes." He waved at Ivy and went out.

Jack touched her softly on the arm and headed for the den; he left her standing alone.

"Okay, kids. TV off. Five minutes with the fish, and that's it for tonight." He spoke to them firmly, but with respect. Ivy liked him for it.

The children obeyed immediately and jockeyed for position at the tank; Jack pushed buttons on a panel, activating some new colored lights and dimming others.

Suddenly Jack bent over and began tapping the small area where a single fish was segregated from the main tank.

"Morris. . . . Wake up, Morris! You're supposed to be vicious!" He turned to the children. "Who's been overfeeding Morris again? He's totally lethargic."

117

"But he's *always* hungry, Jack," the littlest girl said.

"Piranhas are supposed to be hungry," he explained patiently. "A well-filled piranha becomes just another lazy fish."

"I never saw a pet piranha before." Ivy bent over for a closer look.

"It's a lesson to everyone what it's really like . . . out there . . . in the jungle of life." He was very serious, and she moved to him. Jack turned to the children: "Five minutes, that's all." Then he took Ivy's hand: "You come with me."

Jack led her down the hall to his bedroom.

"This house . . . ?" Ivy wondered.

"We own it. Par-Tal does, anyway."

Jack opened the door and ushered Ivy into a spacious room dominated by the huge canopied bed in the center flanked by several deep, well-padded, comfortable-looking chairs. He seated Ivy in one and moved into his dressing room.

"Are these children yours?" Ivy asked.

"Not any of them." Jack's voice was harsh.

"Got any kids of your own?" she asked.

Jack returned to the bedroom with his trousers on and a dress shirt in his hand. "No," he said. He paused, looking at her thoughtfully. His voice softened: "This shirt check out with you? Ironingwise, I mean? I changed laundries." He held it for her inspection.

"It's pretty good, I guess," she said, after examining it.

Jack put the shirt on. "But you could do better . . . ?"

Ivy nodded and Jack nodded too. "Sure . . . first you press my shirts, then you marry me." He crossed to the tie rack and made a selection.

"I'm not sure I even want to go out with you."

"Why?" Jack asked, genuinely surprised. Why should she go to all that trouble to *not* go out with me? he wondered.

"You sure don't seem to want to go out with *me*," Ivy said.

He shook his head. "No. Not right. It's just I didn't think I'd work tonight," he said honestly.

"What kind of truck-driving do you do dressed like that?"

Jack looked at her, startled. "You mean you don't know?"

"Know *what*?" she asked.

Jack collected his coveralls and started to pull them on over his dress clothes. Ivy watched him, waiting for an explanation, and when Jack didn't answer she got up and headed for the door. "I'm going to the movies. Goodnight."

Jack was struggling with the work jumper. "Wait a minute. . . ." He followed her awkwardly. "Look, I called and asked you to go out and so I'll take you out!"

They were back in the living room.

"But you don't want to," she said reasonably.

He looked at her eyes and the neckline of her dress and raised a hand to her hair. "I want to," Jack said. He remembered the children and turned to the tank. "Okay, kids. Put the lights out, Toddy." He opened the door for them, the children said their goodnights, and a little girl curtsied to Ivy; Toddy, the smallest boy, proudly turned off the lights in the fish tank and scampered out after the others.

Jack checked: everyone was ready to go, assembled in the main hallway, the croupiers, dealers, waitresses, all dressed and waiting patiently by the elevator.

Jack beckoned to Ivy. She stood stubbornly for a few seconds before moving.

"All right," she said finally. "But I wouldn't press your shirts if you got on your knees and begged!"

She joined Jack at the door, reluctantly, looking up into his laughing face—and he grew hard again and slowly turned her toward the contingent in the hall. She looked at them, waiting by the elevator for a full minute.

"Say," she said, turning back to him, "what kind of place *is* this?"

Chapter Ten

The ride to Queens was a strained affair. Ivy sat quietly in the middle of the wide back seat, ankles crossed, staring straight ahead through the front windshield, while Billy talked incessantly on her left and Jack stared pointedly out his side window, arm crossed tightly across the front of his coveralls.

"Around the horn or crosstown?" Eddie asked.

"Crosstown," Billy said. "There isn't much traffic."

Eddie headed the limousine for the Queens Midtown Tunnel and Billy directed a monologue at Ivy about the way the West Side Highway passed *right around* the tip of Manhattan to detour the incredibly unscientific layout of the Wall Street section. He was cataloguing the worse bottlenecks by name, enjoying her attempt to appear interested, when they entered the fluorescent light of the tunnel and he made the mistake of glancing at Jack. Billy broke off suddenly and began to whistle softly under his breath.

The gambling truck was backed up against the Par-Tal loading platform, the yard looking silent and abandoned for the night; the purr of the limousine sounded loud and unnatural in the quiet. Eddie blinked the lights and drove slowly forward, waiting for the garage doors to open.

Jack liked to remind himself that a good percentage of Par-Tal Trucking was legitimate; the daytime operations were based in the Queens warehouse and even now the morning shipments were stacked, waiting for the night to pass. But an efficiency expert would have rung his hands in glee, anticipating a fat consultant's fee for eliminating the duplication of work; often at night it was necessary to transfer waiting cargo to make room for the passenger-filled limousines that used the garage at night. And as Eddie pulled their car into a temporary space, Jack looked angrily at the displaced shipment that had been moved very sloppily, the priority boxes buried near the bottom. He helped Ivy out of the limousine and scowled darkly at his partner, pointing at the pile with an angry shake of his head. Billy straightened out of the car and happily redirected Jack's gaze to the open door of the casino.

Their's had been the last car to leave the apartment

building, and the final preparations were almost completed when Jack took Ivy's arm and led her up the red-carpeted ramp.

He stopped to introduce her to the girls standing in the doorway. Edna and Norma were wearing very short, very revealing plastic dresses, their long legs gracefully taut in high-heeled sandals. They moved to let Jack lead Ivy into the truck where the dealers were at their places, counting chips and checking supplies.

She looked, unblinking, from table to table.

They watched Jack lead Ivy up the ramp and disappear into the truck.

"Yes, sir," Billy said. "That there is one prime example of a plain maid."

"Lay off, man," Jerry said, laughing. "Okay, so I was wrong. But imagine being blackmailed into handling that!"

"Can't," Billy said. "Can't imagine it—and can't handle it either!"

"Well," Jack said. "Welcome to the other side of Par-Tal."

Ivy shook her head. "I don't believe it."

Jack looked around the inside of the converted truck. "Sometimes I don't believe it either," he murmured softly. Abruptly he checked his watch. "Almost time for the action," he said.

Jack caught Harry's eyes and pointed to his watch; they waited while he retrieved a clipboard from the back.

"Three minutes," Harry called, alerting the dealers as he walked to the door and stationed himself behind Edna and Norma. "All set," he said.

"C'mon." Jack took Ivy by the arm, led her back down the ramp and quickly removed his coveralls, hanging them on a wall hook and smoothing down his dinner jacket. Billy and Jerry were laughing near the door of the warehouse; Jack called to them, pointing at his watch. They headed out for the cab of the truck, leaving the door open for a limousine that stopped at the foot of the ramp near Jack and Ivy. A middle-aged woman waited for the other two passengers to walk up the ramp before letting the chauffeur help an elderly couple from the car.

"Good evening, Mrs. Kling. Nice to see you." Jack sounded very sincere.

She giggled and smiled happily. "Jack, these are those *wonderful* parents of mine I've mentioned so often. All the way from New Orleans. Mr. and Mrs. Vidal." Her voice was soft with an exaggerated southern accent undaunted by twenty years in New York. "How do you do?" Jack acknowledged the introduction formally and quickly signalled Edna to assist Mrs. Kling's father: a frail wrinkled man in his eighties, his skin mottled with the brown blotches of age, Mr. Vidal eagerly clasped her arm.

"Just set me by the dice table, honey," he chortled. "Put me with the other high rollers."

"That's right, just go right along, Daddy," Mrs. Kling said. "They'll take care of you *fine*." She took her mother's arm and walked up the ramp. Harry checked them off on the list and Norma ushered them inside.

As if on cue another limousine drove into the garage. Jack greeted three couples by name and they stopped to chat before walking up to Harry.

Ivy stood at Jack's side, slightly behind him, watching silently as limousines pulled into the garage at three minute intervals. Most carried a complement of five or six, although one had been specially equipped to transport an elderly woman in a wheel chair. Wrapped in a blanket despite the pleasant warmth of the night, she was pushed up the ramp by a soft-faced young man wearing a diamond ring on each hand and an elaborate Florentine medallion under his unbuttoned Nehru jacket.

"Her husband left her almost seven million dollars," Jack said. "And she doesn't know what to do with it. So she keeps that fop as a companion and pays him a hundred grand a year plus bonuses."

Ivy shook her head. "That's a lot of money."

"Yup," Jack agreed. "But not enough. She comes here at least three times a week with her widowed sisters. She buys their chips and her own and the fop's, too, and they all lose heavily. And she still doesn't come close to spending the *interest* on her money."

He smiled at Ivy in anticipation. "And wait until you see the sisters. They'll be along in the next batch."

Ivy barely managed to suppress an audible laugh as the two women, pink scalps shining through thin, blue-tinged white hair were escorted up the ramp by Harry who met them at the car. They were portly identical twins, ludicrously wearing identical full-length dresses that hiked slightly, when they walked, to reveal bright red space shoes.

Another limousine emptied the only three younger couples into the truck; Harry checked them in and signalled that the house was full.

"Ready to roll?" Jack asked.

"I guess so," Ivy said, prepared to accept anything as possible.

"You really didn't know about this?" It was more of a statement than a question.

"I don't know if I believe what I see even now," she said.

Jack grinned and took her arm.

"But I guess I should say I'm sorry," Ivy said wryly.

"What for?"

"There's nothing two-bit about *your* hustle."

It was a full five seconds before he started to laugh; putting an arm around her waist, Jack led Ivy up the ramp.

Harry closed the doors, signalled the truck's cab for Jerry to move it out and took over the craps table nearest the radiophone and intercom.

"Ivy, I've got work to do," Jack said softly. "I'm sorry."

"I understand." She looked around with interest. "I'd like to watch, if there's somewhere I won't be in the way."

Jack motioned to Norma, and Ivy followed her through the truck. He watched until she was settled against the back wall in the high chair overlooking the action before he moved to the table.

"Harry," he said quietly. "I may want a pick-up at midnight. Tell Eddie to use my car and call in here at eleven thirty."

"Right."

He started for the phone as Jack temporarily took over the table.

"And Harry . . . don't relay the message to Billy up front. Call Eddie yourself from back here."

Between the two Par-Tal decoys, at the wheel of the gambling truck, Jerry final-checked the route with the other drivers. He signed off the phone and turned up the volume on a transistor radio hung from his window visor. They formed a close convoy in the right-hand lane, paced at a steady forty-five. On the seat next to him, awake and fingering money in a cashbox, Billy lost count for the third time and temporarily abandoned his task. He reached up and turned down the volume.

"You should have seen his face in the tunnel," he said, laughing loudly. "And she sat there *listening!*"

"Man, he'll thank you in the morning. That is no one-night-only chick—*unless,* of course, you have a partner that makes you work every night," Jerry said.

"I'd say ol' Jack boy is mighty lucky on that score, wouldn't you?"

"With you around I'm surprised every time he scores, period."

Billy laughed. He turned the volume back up, re-opened the cashbox and started from the beginning, counting slowly. He was almost to the bottom of the pile of bills when Jerry vaguely sensed a siren scream behind them. He turned down the volume. Billy looked up in disgust and slowly abandoned his count; he closed the box and slipped it behind the sliding security panel they had installed in the door.

The siren grew steadily louder and they watched a police car speed by, red light flashing.

Jerry turned up the volume and Billy retrieved the box.

"Must be some lawbreakers abroad," Billy said.

Jerry nodded in agreement. "Must be," he said.

"Place your bets, ladies and gentlemen. Everyone a winner," Jack said jovially.

He riffled the cards with great dexterity and suddenly glanced up at Ivy, sitting nearby against the wall. He caught her watching him intently; she moved a bit, self-consciously, but her answering smile was warm.

Jack cut the deck with riverboat flips, passing it for a final cut and started dealing the hand. He raised his voice slightly so she could hear easily.

"And a little old jack for Jack," he said, putting a cadence in the words. He dealt the up cards.

"Double down on the ten, Mrs. Wetherell? *That's* the old spirit." He dealt her cards. "Stay with the queen and a hit on the seven. Stay with that? Okay. . . . And no hit for Mr. Willis?" He waited for him to make up his mind. "Mrs. Kling, that's a *hand-*some king for you. . . ." She signalled for another card. "And you will stay with that *three*, young lady? My-my!"

Jack dealt himself one card and a moan went up from the table.

"How do you like that!" he said. "Twenty-one." Jack swept in the chips.

"Keep playing, folks. You'll have your revenge from me later," he said, turning the table back to the dealer.

Detouring around the tables, he headed over to Ivy. "Bored?"

"No." She shook her head. "I just wish I understood how to play those games."

"Don't feel bad. A lot of them don't understand the

ones they're playing, either." Jack laughed, shaking his head at the gamblers.

Ivy hesitated for a moment. "I do know a little about dice. And I have ten dollars. . . ."

"You're not allowed," he said firmly.

"Why?"

"We don't take from blood."

Ivy turned down his offer of coffee or a drink and followed him with her eyes, relaxed and intrigued with his easy manner, admiring the way he moved through the truck, stopping at each table to say a few words, charming and elegant. He was wending his way back to her when Edna intercepted him.

"Billy's on the horn," she said. "Says it's important." He nodded and followed her.

"Eddie's checking in," Billy said. "Did you call for a pick-up?"

"Yeah, Billy." Jack checked his watch and glanced over at Ivy.

She was watching the roulette table, bending forward in the chair, her hair falling softly around her face.

In the cab Billy held the phone away from his ear and rolled his eyes at Jerry. "Well?" he asked into the phone.

"I'm thinking. I'm thinking," Jack said. Ivy shifted in the chair and he caressed her thoughtfully with his eyes.

"Listen to loverboy Billy. If you have to think about it, don't do it."

"Amen," said Jerry.

"Jerry says 'Amen,'" Billy told Jack.

"Maybe you're right," he said softly, shifting his gaze from Ivy's legs to her face. She was smiling at him. "And so . . . tell Eddie to pick us up at midnight," Jack told him.

"Why?" Billy wailed.

"Why? Because I can handle her, that's why." He hung up the phone and headed back across the room, stopping to alert Harry to take over.

Billy replaced the receiver under the dash. "Jack says he can handle her," he said solemnly to Jerry.

They laughed for a long time.

"C'mon," he said, offering his hand. "We're leaving."

"Leaving?"

"That's right. Unless, of course, you have another date. . . ." Jack broke off, waiting for her.

"We're leaving," Ivy said, clasping his hand and climbing down from her perch. He led her to the panel and they pushed through awkwardly into the space behind the cab seat.

"You're twenty minutes early, man," Billy said irritably. "Keep down, will you?" He reached for the phone and called the decoy drivers. "Pace it for a midnight drop-off at the first exit after Longworth

131

Road, guys. Over and out." He turned back to Jack. "Eddie said midnight, sharp. We may be ten early ourselves." He nodded to Ivy.

She whispered to Jack, pointing to Jerry. "I saw him in the elevator at your apartment building, but we haven't been introduced."

Jack tapped him on the shoulder. "Jerry, this is Ivy Moore, and you saw her in the elevator, she says, so you can keep your eyes on the road."

"Hi," he said cheerfully. "Glad to meet you."

"Hello, Jerry." She twisted, uncomfortable in the small space, and Jack leaned back against the panel, pulling her with him, supporting her weight easily with one arm. Ivy relaxed against his warm strength, surprisingly comfortable.

Billy stared straight ahead, questioning Jack on the evening's action as they moved steadily behind the lead Par-Tal truck; finally they pulled off at the exit.

"We're early. Eddie's not here yet," Jerry said, carefully braking the truck to a stop. Billy got out of the cab and looked around; he signalled that the way was clear and Jack helped Ivy over the front seat. Then they were standing on the gravel shoulder of a tree-shaded road. A soft breeze carried the scent of damp, rich earth and she shivered slightly in the cool late-night air, bathed in the soft glow of a three-quarter moon.

The trucks moved off quickly, the grind of shifting gears shattering the night, lingering even after the last red taillights blinked around a bend in the road.

Jack looked at his watch. "Eddie should be here in a few minutes."

"I hope he's late," Ivy said. "I like it here. There's something very nice about being stranded like this." She searched for the words. "It's like running away from home when I was ten—going far enough to feel new dirt under my feet, but not so far that I'd really get lost." She laughed softly. "I sure got whopped for that one. But it was worth it anyway."

"Did you run away often?"

"No," she said. "That was the only time." She pulled a leaf from the tree behind them and rubbed it between her fingers, holding it to her nose to smell the freshness of it. "We were very poor. There's no place for a poor colored girl to run to in Florida." She thought a minute. "Unless you want to count my coming north with the Austins." She shivered again and Jack wrapped her in his arms, gently pressing her head against his chest. She nestled there, soft and yielding against his hard body.

Chapter Eleven

"Will you want me later?" Eddie unlocked the front door and handed Jack his keys.

"Maybe." He looked at Ivy thoughtfully; his jacket was hanging loosely from her shoulders and she had grown suddenly quiet.

"Okay," Eddie said. "If I go out, I'll stay close and leave a number with the truck."

Jack shook his head. "No. Phone it in to the switchboard here," he told him. "And take the limousine. I may want my car. You can knock off at four if I don't call."

The night attendant rang for an elevator as Jack guided Ivy across the entrance hall, keeping step with the staccato click of her heels against the marble floor.

"Hello, John. How's the wife?"

"Fine, sir. I'll tell her you asked."

Jack introduced Ivy and the old man politely shook her hand; he held the rubber-edged elevator door firmly while they entered.

"Eddie may phone a number in to you later," Jack said. "Oh, and John, no switchboard calls and no visitors on ten. I'm not home for anyone. And that *includes* Billy."

"I understand. Goodnight, sir . . . Miss Moore." John inserted a key in the small lock below the floor-button panel before he allowed the door to slither shut.

"The door mechanism jams and the elevator automatically heads for the basement at night if someone tries to stop the car at ten without unlocking that gizmo," he explained. "There's an alarm light for the building guard on every floor. He just lets anyone caught in the elevator sweat it out for three or four hours and unless there's some stolen stuff from another floor on him we let him go. The guard is a big, touchy guy. A ex-fighter. He's very mean." Jack turned to face her and grinned. "Remember that if you decide to drop in some time unexpectedly."

Ivy nodded solemnly; in the bright light she avoided his eyes, intent on the steady sweep of the indicator arrow that pointed halfway to eleven before stopping. They stepped out into uncompromising silence; the open doors offered empty rooms, and even the radiophones were idle, helpless with no one to operate them. Ivy thought she could hear her heart beat; the elevator waited for the soft sound of its closing door and the final click as it shut, before descending. Walking hesitantly at Jack's side through the impersonal corridor, she held his dinner jacket closed with both hands until he pushed open the unlocked door and ushered her in with an exaggerated gesture and a slight bow.

Ivy headed across the living room to a deep-cushioned chair and sat down to relieve the weakness in her legs, making herself small, clutching the beaded bag and white gloves firmly in her lap. Body motionless, deliberately looking at her hands, she felt vulnerable and unsure.

Jack forced her to look up at him, standing so close she could feel the warmth of his body, waiting easily as she slowly raised her head. He studied her face for a long time before gently reclaiming his jacket from her shoulders. His hand softly traced the left side of her face, the line of her neck.

"Would you like something?" He unclasped her hands to take the purse and gloves.

"No. I don't drink." She managed a weak smile.

Jack carried her things to a cabinet under the children's drawings and returned with a decanter and two large snifters.

"Neither do I," he said. "Except religiously once a year. After a Thursday night tryst with a beautiful woman on a lonely country road . . . and a chilly ride home without my jacket."

"It's Friday morning," she said softly.

He handed her a glass and poured them each a small brandy. "To Friday morning, then," he toasted. "Thanks for helping me break out of the rut. A routine like that . . . it gets deadly after a while!"

They clinked glasses. The brandy burned into her —and suddenly Ivy was herself again as the comfort of the room and the warmth of Jack's smile shattered her uneasiness. Slowly, unconsciously, her body relaxed in the chair.

And she watched him happily, sipping her brandy carefully as he selected and threaded a tape, adjusting the controls to spill easy, lyrical jazz softly from the speakers. And she watched him play with the fish tank lights for a long time, changing colors and intensities until finally, after she had wandered to the near doorway, he was satisfied and flicked the panel's master switch: the fish tank came alive as the living room lights blinked off in unison.

"It's down the hall," Jack said, pointing.

"Oh, no, I was looking for the kitchen." She walked to his side, staring with delight at the tank.

"Why?"

She shrugged her shoulders. "I'd just like to see it," she said simply.

"Okay." Jack took Ivy's hand to lead her through the darkened dining room, releasing it to switch on the kitchen light. He leaned comfortably against the doorpost as she slowly admired the immaculate room.

Why, this kitchen is more efficiently arranged than the Austins', she thought. She peeked into the oven and ran a finger over the chrome trim on the cabinets.

"Somebody really keeps it clean," she said, glancing at him quickly, then peering into the toaster.

"Jerry's mother comes in, so I can't use you." Amusement played with the corners of his mouth.

She looked up quickly. "I don't intend doing that anymore except for myself." She was very earnest and held her head high, cocked slightly to one side.

He reached out for her hand. "Okay, then, let's go." He settled her on the couch facing the fish tank, carelessly rolling up his sleeves and kicking off his shoes. He sat down close to her, so close they touched; he reached for the cigarette box on the table.

Ivy beat him to it, carefully raising one to his lips. Jack crossed his arms, leaning back, as she removed a small wax match from the box and held it, lit and shielded with her hand. He looked at her thoughtfully, letting the flame burn down dangerously low in her fingers before he moved to use the light. She discarded the spent match in the large, heavy glass ashtray on the table.

He watched her enjoy the fish gliding through the water, noted the motion of her dress as she responded

to the smooth rhythm of the music; she seemed unaware of his eyes on her until he shifted slightly to
lean to the table. Suddenly she picked up the ashtray
and held it out to him.

"Leave that!" Jack's voice was angry. He pulled it
away and replaced it on the table.

"You'd let me hold it if I were Japanese," she said
reasonably.

"Well, you're *not* Japanese." He flicked his cigarette, missing it altogether, scattering ashes on the
table. "You're a twenty-eight-year-old colored girl
looking to get married!"

"I'm twenty-seven," Ivy said. "And why do you
keep saying that?"

"Because I'm a thirty-six-year-old colored man looking to stay single!"

He viciously snubbed out his cigarette, the un-
smoked tobacco spilling into the ashtray from the
shredded paper. He toyed with it absently. Well, do I
make a move or don't I, he wondered, resettling
against the back of the couch. She turned to face him,
her dress pulling high above her knees. He glanced at
her legs. I make a move, he thought.

"Is it true they give you baths?" she asked suddenly.

He looked up. "Who gives who baths?"

"Japanese girls."

"I shower twice a day . . . by myself."

Ivy pulled off her shoes and tucked her legs up under her on the seat.

"I hear it's fun taking a shower with someone," she said. "I've never done that."

"Obviously you go with unsanitary men." The music stopped and their voices seemed louder than before.

"I don't go with anybody!"

Her angry pout amused him and he reached over to turn up the corners of her mouth with his hand, waiting until she smiled easily before getting up to change the tape.

Jack settled back against the arm of the couch, bracing himself to reach for her.

"Why don't you put your feet up and get comfortable?" she asked, quickly getting up. "You've been standing all night. I could rub your feet."

He stopped her from kneeling on the floor. "I can rub my own feet. And I would, if they hurt . . . which they don't."

She eluded his arms and walked to the fish tank. "Just like color TV," she said brightly. "Or like home." She tapped the glass with her finger, moving slowly around the tank until he told her to stop; he slid an arm tightly around her waist when she obeyed.

"When I was little I used to go fishing with my gramma," she said, testing his grip with a pressure of her body. "Sometimes it was the only food we had."

Jack bent down and softly nuzzled her ear, running

his lips slowly down to rest against the pulse beat at the side of her neck.

"Do you ever go home?" she asked weakly.

"No."

"I don't either," Ivy said, forcing a strained laugh as he led her back to the couch.

"There's a big orange-juice canning factory where my gramma's house used to be." She dragged her feet and sighed with unconscious but audible relief when he let go of her waist and sat down.

But suddenly before she could move, he reached up and took both her hands, pulling her firmly down to the couch.

"Can I get you some cookies?" Her voice sounded strange to her ears.

And he shook his head no and with strong arms twisted her around, forcing her legs up on the couch. Gently, slowly, he drew her rigid body closer, cradling her head on his shoulder and supporting her against him with an arm, his free hand toying with her hair. He kissed her eyes shut and softly kissed her closed lips, caressing the smooth skin of her upper arm. He nibbled her ear and ran his tongue lightly down her neck to the hollow of her shoulder, and felt her shiver as he moved back to her mouth.

And then Ivy went soft against him and slowly began to move, a hand shyly reaching for the back of his neck as she opened to the sweet kiss.

He drew her hard against him, hands moving on

her back as she locked her arms behind his neck and returned the kiss, her body moving, demanding now, a soft noise from her throat.

Then, with a sudden, horrible clarity, Jack knew it was almost too late—for his mind showed him a picture of the future with Ivy ironing his shirt, and it triggered a hidden reserve of strength. Slowly he broke her hold on his neck and sat her up, away from him, avoiding her eyes; he reached for a cigarette. She quickly lit a match.

He rolled down his sleeves. I must be out of my *mind*, he thought. One look at her and I *knew:* she's *the* domestic. It isn't *worth* it.

He slipped on his shoes. "You know, I think it's about time I sent you home."

"There's no hurry," she said. "Tomorrow's my day off."

He was in control again, and he looked at her. "Well, I have to work day *and* night."

Ivy settled into the cushions. "When you're put in jail, can I bring you cookies?"

"That's not very funny." He switched on the table lamp at his side and retrieved the jacket he had thrown on a chair.

"Will it be funny if you're caught?"

"I knew it—a reformer!" Thank you, baby, he thought, you're making it easier. Keep it up.

"I'm not." She watched him struggle into his jacket,

142

and a sudden feeling of despair welled up in her. "I'm not anything," she said softly. "That's the trouble."

"Wrong," he said. "You're something, all right." Really something, he thought.

"But you don't want me. So I can't be very much." She toyed with the polish on her left thumbnail.

"And what if I did want you?"

"I guess I wouldn't mind." Her voice was soft.

"What's the matter with you!" He walked angrily to the couch. "Do you just throw yourself at *anybody?*"

Ivy shook her head and refused to look up. "You're not just anybody."

"That's right! You *said* I'm not a two-bit hustler, didn't you!" He put out his cigarette and paced the room until he spotted her bag and gloves. He grabbed them and walked over to toss them beside her on the couch.

"I'm going to call Eddie," he said moving to the phone. "He can ride you around a while before taking you home."

He made the mistake of looking at her, sitting head bowed and vulnerable, and he slowly replaced the receiver. He walked to the couch. "You said you wouldn't mind if I wanted. Why?"

"Because I like you." Her voice was muffled.

"That shows how wrong you are." He quickly lifted her face with his hand. "You see that fish?" He pointed to the separate cage in the tank. "That piranha strikes at everything that gets in its way.

143

That's me. And with little chicks like you, I'm *murder*." He pushed her against the back of the couch and leaned over her, resting a hand on either side, bringing his face close. "There's bodies strewn all *over* this city!"

"I'll bet there are." Her voice was stronger now; her eyes met his evenly.

"You better believe it!" He waved his arm in emphasis and started back to the phone.

Ivy quickly slipped into her shoes and got up. "You don't have to call anybody. I'll get the bus."

"*Oh* no you won't!" he yelled. "I'm not going through *that* bit again, seeing you sitting alone in that miserable place." He puffed out his cheeks and shook his head. "You're not giving *me* guilt, baby."

She took the receiver from his hand and replaced it in the cradle. "I'm *not* going home in a limousine."

"Okay . . . okay . . . so *I'll* drive you home. I'll even lend you a jacket so I can keep mine on."

"I don't want you to take me home."

Jack crossed to the front closet and noisily pulled hangers across the bar; he came up with a long coat sweater and opened the door to the outside hall. "Ready?"

Ivy walked to him slowly. "Why'd you even bring me here?"

"Temporary insanity. The *last* thing I want is to get involved."

She nodded her head. "Okay. I understand. You

don't have to see me anymore." It was a simple solution, and she offered it to him honestly.

"What kind of talk is that?" He held the sweater for
her; neither noticed the inside-out sleeve until she
awkwardly turned to look for the opening.

And suddenly her face was buried against his chest.
"But I do *like* you!" She sounded lost and small, and
without thinking his arms were around her, his mouth
reaching for hers, and he bit at her nose playfully and
closed his eyes and kissed her again. Her arms went
around his neck and he saw her cooking in his
kitchen and with a last gasp he broke her grip and
thrust her away.

"Now, *look . . . !*"

She stood framed in the light from the hall, the
sweater hanging ridiculously from one shoulder, looking beautiful and desirable . . . and very undomestic.
And with a sudden uncontrollable passion he kicked
the door shut and threw the latch, leaning against it
and reaching out for her.

"Oh, the *hell* with it," he said as she walked slowly
into his open arms.

And he crushed her to him and kissed her until he
felt her legs give way.

The last limousine filled with customers had left the
garage more than an hour before and the gambling
casino was backed against the outside wall, hemmed
in by two disabled trucks. Billy and Jerry were still

145

working with the dealers to restack the cargo in shipping order, checking the crate numbers against the
master list Harry now held in his clipboard. They
were almost done.

Edna and Norma dozed in the back seat of a limousine, a thin blanket protecting them from the early
morning chill. It had been a long night.

"Okay, Billy, it checks out," Harry said, rubbing his
eyes. "Let's knock off." He tossed the clipboard on a
crate. "One of these days we're going to come up with
a better system . . . I *hope*."

"Yeah," Billy said. "I'll just talk Jack into giving up
the daytime action, ha . . . ha . . . !" He
stretched and yawned loudly.

Jerry slumped against a wall, exhausted. "Not a bad
idea, man. This physical labor is just *too* much. No
one has the strength left to *move* even!"

"Yeah? Watch this." Billy cupped a hand around
his mouth. "Okay, you guys," he yelled. "That's it.
Let's knock it off for the night."

Like a horde of hungry locusts, the dealers gratefully headed for the cars.

"If they moved like that to work we'd be out of
here in ten minutes flat every night," Jerry said, grinning.

"Yeah, *wouldn't* we!"

The cars moved out and Billy took a final look-see
inspection before heading for the warehouse office;

146

the evening's receipts were in the cashbox under his arm.

He removed an ordinary drain from the concrete floor and pushed the button that activated the lift for a small, heavy safe. He looked at it fondly, pleased as he was every night with the genius of his invention. He opened the safe, emptied the cashbox into a manila envelope and noted that it was almost time to send off a package to their Swiss banker.

It was a cheerful thought and he whistled all the way back to the car.

For once Jerry didn't object: he was very tired and it helped keep him awake at the wheel. But soon Billy stopped, resting his head against the seat, dozing comfortably.

Jerry cursed softly, narrowly missing a car as he inadvertently ran a red light; he was flagged down by a cop. The other cars are back home and they's all asleep, he thought. Billy is asleep. Jack is asleep. Everyone in the whole *world* is asleep but me and this damn cop.

He handed over his license and registration and waited for the ticket. Billy exhaled a loud snore and turned over on his side.

Jerry shook him awake when they got home. He held the door open, and headed for the elevator while Billy scuffled to the switchboard to report to Jack; Jerry waited, listening to the conversation and shaking his head to clear his ears.

147

"You're last in," John said, handing Billy the elevator key. "You leave it open."

"Ring him, will you, John?"

"I'm sorry, Mr. Talbot, but Mr. Parks left orders that he wasn't in for anyone."

"Yeah, okay. But ring him for me anyway like you do every night."

John looked miserable as he shook his head. "I'm sorry, sir, but he *specifically* mentioned that he wasn't home to anyone . . . including you. He mentioned you by *name*, Mr. Talbot. So I'm sorry, but I can't ring him."

Billy ran his tongue over his lips. "What time did he get in?"

"About one o'clock or a little later maybe."

"Was he alone?" Billy asked, reading the answer.

John hesitated.

"Well, was he?"

John looked down and avoided Billy's eyes. "Well . . . no, sir, he wasn't . . ."

"I don't believe it," Billy said slowly. He signalled Jerry over to the desk. "Did you hear?"

"I heard," Jerry said. "And I don't believe it either. For the love of . . . he said he could handle her!"

He looked back at John. "Was it Miss Moore?"

John nodded.

"Maybe he sent her home with Eddie and just decided to get a good night's sleep," Jerry offered tentatively, looking at Billy with a worried expression.

They turned to John. He shook his head slowly. "No, sir, Eddie left a call number here with me and he went off duty at four like Mr. Parks said he could if he wasn't needed."

"I don't suppose he took her home himself?" Billy asked hopefully, knowing the answer without hearing it. "Yeah, well . . . okay. See you tomorrow night."

He followed Jerry to the elevator, watched him push seven and then pushed ten. "Christ," he said. "Why can't he just go out, nice and simple, without getting involved with a chick who has *nice and respectable* written all over her?"

"Yeah," Jerry said. "Why can't he?"

"Oh, shut up," Billy said irritably. "I asked you first."

The elevator stopped at seven and Jerry said goodnight, hurrying now for the waiting softness of his bed. The door shut, and Billy leaned against the wall thinking, remembering with horror the Kyoto jail he had called home in Japan because of Jack and a nice, respectable girl; he shuddered and quickly suppressed the thought.

The pointer passed ten and moved halfway to eleven; the elevator shuddered to a stop, groaned slightly and plummeted for the basement. Billy looked stupidly at the small key in his hand.

He sank down onto the floor. It figures, he thought. This has turned out to be one hell of a lousy night. He wondered idly how long it would take for the night watchman to come around, then he rested his head on the wall and loudly began to snore.

Ivy sat on the window sill wrapped in his short Japanese lounging coat, hugging her knees and looking out into the first gray morning light. The George Washington Bridge was almost without traffic, its night lights beginning to lose their sharpness with the dawn. A few cars passed on the West Side Highway below, evenly divided between uptown and down, but soon there was a trickle and across the Palisades she caught quick glimpses of house lights coming on. The downtown, into-Manhattan traffic began to increase.

She strained to see the limousine that stopped at the front door, unable to identify the passengers because of the angle and the still feeble light. But another drove up, and a third and the street lights suddenly flicked out and it was morning. She recognized Jerry and Billy easily because they parked their car and walked across the street.

She turned suddenly and looked at Jack, asleep under a sheet, and her happiness welled up into a full smile, her eyes misting slightly and crinkling at the corners. She watched him for a long time, hunching tightly over her knees, and finally she pulled her eyes away and looked leisurely around the room wondering what she would like to change. She had just decided to re-upholster the small chair when he called out.

"Hey . . . you!"

She looked over at him guiltily.

He was leaning on an elbow looking at her, the sheet pulled down to his waist and a new wave of pleasure overwhelmed her; she leaned back against the window wall for support.

"What're you doing over there?" he asked. "Especially when you can be over here." He patted the sheet with his hand.

She laughed and ran to him, burying her head on his chest, nibbling at him, leaning back to let him loosen the robe.

"You were asleep," she said, running a finger down his arm. "And I couldn't sleep. It's so quiet here." She moved sensuously beneath his hands. "At the Austins' there's one bobwhite drives me crazy, but I'm so used to it and I guess it'll take some doing to *un*-get used to it."

"I'll get you a dozen of them for Christmas," he said. "Any color you want."

She laughed happily with the nearness of him and the joy of her body and the thought of a dozen colored bobwhites.

"Your people just got home. I saw them from the window."

He slipped the robe from her shoulders and looked

151

at her slowly. "Somehow I'd rather be doing this," he said.

"Go back to sleep," Ivy said, laughing. "It's still very early."

He covered her gently with the sheet, caressing her lightly, changing her laugh into a deep, content sigh and she nestled easily against him.

"I ought to be thinking about getting you home," he said, mussing her hair, her body feeling incredibly soft and smooth against him.

"I told you . . . it's my day off."

"Isn't that nice?" he said gently, leaning over. Isn't she beautiful, he thought, and he pulled her toward him harshly, kissing her slowly and deeply, and for a long time.

"Hey!" She pulled away from him suddenly and sat up, the sheet falling to her waist, bending over him.

"What?"

She suddenly looked shy and he kissed the palm of her hand. "Let's take a shower," she said quickly.

He laughed with delight and pulled her down again, almost smothering her with kisses. "Later . . ." he said. "Much later."

Chapter Twelve

Doris quickly buried the notes in a tangle of papers on top of the desk and looked up as her secretary entered.

"It's marked Personal," Marie said, handing her an interdepartment envelope. I'm going to lunch now, Mrs. Austin. Shall I have the switchboard hold calls?"

"Yes. And shut my door on the way out. Have a good lunch."

Doris opened the envelope. It contained an invoice for three dozen size five micro-skirts in assorted colors and across the top of it Frank had scrawled: "*Great!* Next year we can sew on numbers and sell them to miniature golf courses for hole markers! *Has she gone crazy???*" Clipped to the invoice were a handwritten original and typed file-copy of the order—both clearly signed *Gena Austin*. Doris tossed the papers in the TO DO basket and decided to have a talk with her daughter. She retrieved the buried papers.

A half-eaten cheese sandwich and a container of milk were by the phone; she looked at them and grimaced. From her purse she took a shopping list and carefully double-checked it against the recipes she had copied earlier from a *Joy of Cooking* in Books. She had decided to play it safe: fruit cocktail (from a jar), soup (add a little wine to some Campbell's), a roast, potatoes, salad (with bottled dressing) and a frozen cake for dessert. It had been a long time; she hadn't so much as boiled an egg for almost nine years —not since Ivy came. But after all, Doris thought, it's really not all *that* hard. People just don't forget how to cook! She pushed the recipes and shopping list into her purse.

She leaned back in her chair and looked around the office, at the drawing board and untidy stacks of sketches, at the overflowing cork pegboard, at a muslin work copy of a design pinned to a dress form in the corner—the familiar tools of her trade. She drank her milk slowly and nibbled at the sandwich; feeling her determination waver she hastily scribbled a note for Marie that she was going home, asking her to let Frank's secretary know where she was. She phoned and ordered the company car to meet her at the front entrance and not waiting for the elevator she walked the three flights down to the main floor of the department store.

She spotted Gena through the streamers, her back to the door, talking on the wall phone; the car had not yet arrived and Doris threaded her way across the Boutique to ask her daughter about the micro-skirts.

Gena was still on the phone, her voice carrying in the early afternoon lull.

". . . backfired? Ivy isn't even *home* yet? Well, isn't that what we wanted?" she was asking.

Doris looked thoughtfully at her daughter's back. What had backfired?

"Now look, Tim, just because he runs that gambling place doesn't mean . . ." Gena leaned closer to the phone, shielding the mouthpiece with her hand, and Doris strained to hear her, certain she had misunderstood . . . hoping she had misunderstood.

"But it was your idea in the first place! I don't understand why you're so upset . . . Ivy's a grown woman and she seems to really like him. You should be very happy; it looks like it's going to work," Gena said.

Doris grabbed the phone. "What's this all about, Tim?" she asked. "I want an answer right now from both of you." She stared at her daughter, defying her to move away, and waited angrily for Tim's explanation.

Tim dribbled, feinted to the right, pivoted and

drove for the basket, sinking the shot and shouting,
". . . And in goes Alcindor for two big points!" He
looked at his early dusk shadow for approval, retrieved the basketball and dribbled the length of the
concrete pool house court. He was sorting things out
in his head, calmed down finally after the disastrous
talk with his mother. Carefully he weighed it all up
again, silently parrying the objections he knew would
come. Taking each of them in turn, planning his strat-
egy. Yes, he thought. I think it will work.

He threw the basketball from the edge of the grass,
missing the backboard entirely: a car was crunching
up the driveway and he waited expectantly. Frowning, he watched Ivy get out of a big limousine and
talk briefly with the driver before heading for the
house. He returned her wave sullenly and re-evaluated
his plan, looking thoughtfully at the waiting limousine.

The basketball had rolled to a stop against the
metal rung of a pool chair. Tim worked it free with a
nudge from his sandal, and kicked it into the pool. He
pushed his hair back and wiped his forehead on the
torn shirt's sleeve.

Gena had helped her mother with the shopping
after extracting a promise that they would drop the
subject of Ivy, and now an uneasy truce ruled in the
kitchen.

At first Doris had moved about briskly in an at-

156

tempt to look efficient and at home, but she had run into trouble immediately and things were getting worse with alarming speed. And now Gena, her newly-washed hair wrapped in a towel, turned to the phone in her hand to hide her amusement from Doris's wrath at her latest mishap: after rummaging around through half of the kitchen drawers Doris had finally located the meat baster, carried it triumphantly to the oven, opened the door—and reached for the roasting pan bare-handed. With an anguished cry she hurried to the sink and the cold water faucet.

"I wouldn't mind a quiet evening watching the tube myself, Lenny," Gena confided. "Hold it, I'll ask." She looked back at Doris and saw the limousine pulling up through the window. "Mom, Lenny's banished from his house and is too broke to buy dinner. Can I tell him to come here?"

Doris glared up from her damaged fingers. "Tell him to go to the Salvation Army." She pointed through the window. "I suppose that's an *illegal* car."

Gena looked at her, worried. "Mother, I hope you don't . . ."

"And get off that phone!" Doris walked back to the stove in a huff, opening drawers until she found a pot holder. She shook it at her daughter's back. "Employee's picnic! Really, Gena, I don't know how you could have let this thing go so far."

Gena leaned close to the wall and covered the mouthpiece with the cup of her hand, speaking very softly. "Banal panic reigns here, too, luv. Come by at eight thirty. I'll save something cold for you. Mother's having an absolute fit. See you later."

Gena hung up and turned to find Ivy at the back door staring at Doris, her mouth open, unmoving until Doris suddenly slammed the oven door shut, catching Ivy by surprise. She challenged her to laugh with a deadly-set face. But Ivy nodded at her with approval and waved lightly at Gena.

"Hi," Ivy said brightly. "Something smells good." She smiled reassuringly and headed for her room.

"Hey, that's some class!" Gena gestured at the limousine, scurrying after her. "I want to hear all about it!"

"Later! Now you help me get the potatoes on." Doris thrust them at her and started slamming through the drawers, impatiently looking for the peeler.

"I'll help as soon as I change," Ivy offered.

"No . . . no . . ." Doris moved her head slowly with the forbearance of one feeling put upon. "It's still your day off . . . and I guess you have someone waiting." She walked deliberately back to the oven, head held high, and proficiently but unnecessarily re-basted the roast.

Ivy smiled gently at Gena's exaggerated shrug and headed for her room. Gena looked longingly after her. Doris slammed the oven shut and finally located the peeler.

"Get to work, young lady," she said. "Now!"

She left no room for argument and Gena reluctantly took the potatoes to the sink. She retied her robe with an angry knot and started to work.

Doris waited a minute then surreptitiously retrieved her pocketbook from the breakfast table and walked to the hall, pausing for a moment as a muted yell from Frank drifted downstairs. She hesitated; she couldn't make out what he wanted and decided to ignore him, heading for the safety of the hall bathroom to reread the recipes; she was feeling very grim.

Upstairs Frank was fuming, yelling futilely as he angrily tossed through his clothes for the third time. He slammed the closet door in disgust and yelled again loudly, his hands on his hips clenched in tight fists. He took two frustrated steps and stopped, glaring at the closet door.

Doris reached the bathroom just as Tim slammed the front door and came barging into the hall. "Hey, can't you hear? I heard him yelling outside." Tim pointed upstairs. "He wants to know where his gray blazer is."

"Okay, okay!" Doris walked to the bottom of the stairs and yelled: "It's wherever Ivy put it, Frank!" She heard him stamp across the floor to the bathroom and, taking her purse, she headed for the liquor cabinet in the living room and quickly checked the recipe. A cup of sherry and a quarter-cup of heavy cream in the soup, she repeated to herself. Doris stopped suddenly. Or was it the other way around? She found the sherry, stopped to check the recipe again and closed the purse firmly. Through the kitchen door she saw Tim stuff some bills from the emergency envelope on the bulletin board into his pocket and hurry for the back door. Doris broke into a half-run.

"Where are you going?" she demanded, waving her purse at him.

"Downtown for a hamburger." Tim cleared the hair from his forehead.

Doris stamped her foot. "Oh, no you don't. *Oh*, no you don't! I'm making dinner and you'll stay home and eat it." Tim looked at her sullenly and slumped into a chair at the breakfast table, watching her slam the pocketbook on a counter and noisily open soup cans, emptying them into a pot on the stove. Gena finished peeling the potatoes and plopped down opposite him.

"Doris!" Frank bellowed from the top of the stairs, walking halfway down so he could see into the kitchen. "I've looked everywhere! And there's no hot water! No hot water at *all*."

Doris looked at him hopelessly. "It was supposed to be fixed, Frank." He stormed back up the stairs and they shuddered in unison when the bedroom door slammed so hard it sprang back open. He slammed it again.

Gena looked over to Tim. "You catch the limousine bit?"

He nodded gloomily at her and played with the sleeve of his shirt.

"She must've really made out."

Doris whirled around. "I cannot *bear* vulgarity." She glared them into silence and returned, satisfied, to the soup. She gingerly tasted it and groaned silently . . . too much sherry. She had ruined *canned* soup!

"Well, it's not." Frank was suddenly in the kitchen doorway, his voice dangerously low and controlled. Doris had not heard him come down the stairs.

"Not what?" she asked, stirring the soup frantically, as if perhaps that would help.

"*Fixed!*" he yelled. Frank shifted his weight on his feet and thrust his clenched fists into his pockets. "There's no hot water!" He stared at her back. "Have you called the employment agency yet?" he asked nastily, knowing that she had not.

"No." She tasted again; it was still horrible and she added more cream to see if it would help.

Frank walked over to look at the soup, curious. "Don't you think it's time? Why is this house without a maid?"

Doris ignored him and escaped to the refrigerator on an unnecessary errand, rummaging around and moving things from shelf to shelf to avoid the distasteful subject. Gena, rubbing her wet hair with the towel, rolled her eyes at Tim. He smirked and reached into his pocket for a cigarette.

Frank looked at his family with disgust. On an impulse he filled the stirring-spoon and lifted it to his mouth, cautiously blowing to cool the soup. He tasted it tentatively and spit the taste out into the sink. "And why are we eating home on Ivy's night out?" He threw the spoon back into the soup, splattering it on the stove. "What are you trying to prove, Doris?"

She slammed the refrigerator door, holding a bottle of horseradish in her hand and sputtered helplessly as he walked angrily for the liquor cabinet in the dining room.

"And find out where my gray blazer is," he yelled. "I'm going to have a drink. Maybe a whole *bottle!*"

Ivy carefully hung the dress in her closet, looking at it fondly, and changed her underwear. She washed in a hurry—there wasn't any hot water—wrapped her toothbrush in a tissue and carried it back to the little overnight bag open on the bed next to her beige dress.

She was looking through her pile of plain cotton nightgowns when Doris immediately followed her knock on the door into the room. Ivy shut the drawer and carried her brush from the dresser top to the bathroom mirror.

"Ivy, Mr. Austin can't find his gray blazer."

"It'll be back from the cleaner tomorrow."

"And there doesn't seem to be hot water." Doris

walked to the bed and looked at the overnight case, frowning.

"It must be that starter again, Mrs. Austin. You can work it manually." She fussed with her hair happily, tossing it into shape with the brush. Doris sighed and collapsed into a chair.

Ivy looked up and smiled. "I'll do it before I go," she said, turning back to finish straightening her hair. Satisfied, she crossed to the bed and slipped into her dress, smoothed it down and opened the closet door to check in the mirror.

"What a stupid mistake," Doris said suddenly. "I'm so stupid, Ivy." She was looking down, her arms hanging loosely toward the floor. "Such a feeling of . . . *inadequacy*." She was asking for understanding. "I decided . . . well, I ran a house *once*, why couldn't I do it again?"

Ivy nodded at her in agreement. She decided against a nightgown, selected a change of underwear and arranged it neatly in the case.

"It's a disaster, Ivy." Doris had gotten up and stood nervously by the window, playing with the ring on the shade's pull.

"I tell you, that dinner smells *good*," Ivy offered in comfort. "It's just that you're out of the habit, Mrs. Austin."

"No, it's not that, Ivy," Doris said slowly, pacing to the middle of the room, getting in Ivy's way. "It's that

I got to be too *dependent,* Ivy. That's always bad."

Ivy walked around her with a pair of stockings and a clean handkerchief. "I don't know," she said, glancing up from her packing. "Now and then you meet somebody you wouldn't mind depending on."

"Like Mr. Parks?"

Ivy shook her head slowly. "Maybe," she said.

Doris sat down on the bed and toyed with her right earring. Ivy retrieved her hairbrush from the bathroom and final-checked the little bag against the mental list she had compiled in the car.

"You're going out with him again tonight?" Doris asked casually, removing the earring to rub the red mark where it had been.

Ivy nodded and closed the case, clicking the hinged locks into place. "Yes," she said. "Just as soon as I finish. Dinner, a movie, then just . . ." she looked away. "You know." She took a little make-up kit from her purse to the bathroom mirror and carefully went to work on her eyes.

Doris silently watched her work with the lining pencil. Gena and Tim hadn't told her about tonight, and she frowned and turned to go and ask them. She stopped, holding the knob in her hand without turning it.

"Did he ask you out tonight?"

"Well . . . yes." Her view blocked by the closet,

Ivy moved into the room and looked at Doris curiously.

"He *asked* you?"

"Yes. Why?"

Doris shrugged uncomfortably. "Nothing it's just . . ." she broke off and caught at a corner of her bottom lip with her teeth for a moment. "You know . . . if Gena was getting involved like this, she and I would have a long talk . . . that's all."

"Gena always has a lot of choices," Ivy said with a matter-of-fact toss of her head.

Doris watched her with honest concern. "It's simply that I hope you won't get into any trouble, Ivy."

She laughed and went to finish her make-up. "No chance of *that*," she said, checking her eyes in the mirror. "I've got those pills Gena gave me."

"Pills!" Doris sounded horrified. "Gena?" she hurried to the bathroom door.

"She said they were from your prescription," Ivy explained.

"Oh," Doris said, relieved. "But . . . I meant the gambling . . ." She trailed off as Ivy's eyes widened in dismay—they turned in unison as Gena came bursting into the room without knocking.

"Mom, I think the roast . . ."

"*Pills!*" Doris started toward her angrily.

"Mrs. Austin wait!" Ivy started after her, "What do you know about the gambling?"

"Oh, Lord!" Gena moaned, backing up then fleeing

165

from the room. Doris angrily followed after her and Ivy completed the exodus.

Doris grabbed Gena's arm. "What did you have to threaten him with *this* time to get that limousine up here?"

"Mother, please . . ." She shook her arm free and hurried over to Tim at the breakfast table for help. It looked like everything was about to blow up, and she wished she was in Kalamazoo.

"Mrs. Austin." Ivy stationed herself firmly in the middle of the kitchen floor. "What do you know about that gambling truck?"

Doris quickly maneuvered to the breakfast table, horribly aware of the terrible mistake she had made. Gena began vigorously rubbing her hair with the towel, her head lowered toward the floor; Tim slowly and with great deliberation lit a cigarette, his eyes staring at his feet.

Ivy walked over to them angrily. "Won't somebody answer me?" She waited; they pointedly avoided her gaze.

Unexpectedly, Tim bounded from his chair. "Later . . ." he said and headed for the back door, almost colliding with his father who was coming from the dining room with a drink in his hand. Frank held it up protectively as Ivy ran past to block Tim's way.

"Hold it," she said. "You're not going anywhere." She took Tim's arm and walked him back to the table. No one moved.

"I want to know what you all know about Jack Parks," Ivy said. No one would look at her. Furious, she slammed her hand on the table.

"It's not Mom's fault, Ivy," Gena said quickly. "She knew only what we told her."

"Ivy, I just learned today . . ." Doris's voice trailed off.

"What did you learn?" Ivy stared at her, face frozen, waiting for an answer.

"*What's going on?*" Frank walked to Doris's side; they ignored him.

Tim sat down uncomfortably on the edge of the chair. "Look, Ive . . ."

"Do you know about the truck?" Ivy looked from Tim to Gena to Doris.

Frank had a bewildered expression on his face. "Know about what truck?" He looked from Ivy to Gena to his wife.

"Is that how you got him to do it?" Ivy was suddenly feeling sick to her stomach and she braced an arm on the table.

"Got who to do what?" Frank asked.

"Mother, it was *not* any of your business!" Gena sprang from the chair and made a wide circle, flinging her arms wildly; the towel fell from her head into a heap on the floor.

Ivy kicked the towel into a corner. "I suppose it wasn't any of my business either? That's how you did it. . . ." She leaned down to hiss in Tim's ear, and he flinched. "You threatened to tell about the gambling if he didn't take me out. Didn't you?" She scowled at Frank and turned back to Doris. "He *never* wanted to take me out."

"What gambling?" Frank was getting mad. "Where?"

"And the *worst* I figured was he just wanted to stay in good . . ." She ran out of words and moved for the safety of her room; Tim caught her near the sink.

"Ive, you're overreacting," he said, taking her arm.

She shook him off fiercely. "You're supposed to be my *friend.*"

The anger left suddenly, drained away, and in its place the ache was back. Ivy turned back to Tim with her pain. "You're supposed to be my friend," she repeated. "I *trusted* you."

"I *am* your friend," he said slowly.

"That's why we did it." Gena said eagerly, walking over.

"Did *what?*" Frank bellowed, thoroughly bewildered. He looked at his drink and headed for the ice in the refrigerator's freezing compartment. Ivy moved to the door of her room.

She hesitated, head bowed, then slowly straightened up tall, and turned to face them, regaining her dignity. "What did you figure to get out of it?" she asked. "To make me stay here?"

"That's right, Ive . . ." Tim wanted to go to her but he had to respect the look on her face.

Gena ran a hand through her still damp hair. "*That's* why we did it," she said.

"And is that so bad . . . that we love you enough to want you to stay?" Doris asked righteously, extending a supplicating hand.

"That's not why you want me to stay." Ivy's voice was flat.

"Yes it is. We'll even send you to secretarial school." Doris was eager now. "The same way we'd send Gena or Tim to school. Frank and I talked about it, didn't we, Frank?" He had joined the family group and she smiled at him fondly, her voice hopeful and animated. "You can live here and go to school right here in town." She waited, expectant; it would turn out all right.

Ivy looked at Doris thoughtfully. "You don't understand," she said evenly. "I am going to leave and live in the city. I want my own life. I don't *want* to be like Gena and Tim." The whole thing was suddenly intolerable. She withdrew a few steps, very angry, hesitated and turned back to them, angrily. "And I'm leaving *right now*," she yelled. "Tonight!"

Frank moved to her quickly. "Ivy, I want to know what's going on."

"Oh, Frank . . ." Doris wailed.

He whirled around. "Don't *oh, Frank me!*" he screamed; he lowered his voice and turned back to Ivy. "Whatever they did, Ivy, maybe they meant well." He looked at her, thinking it over, and thoughtfully looked at his family. He looked at each of them in turn and they avoided his eyes. "And maybe they didn't," he said slowly.

Ivy looked at him steadily. "Nobody has to blackmail Gena's friends into taking her out," she said simply.

Doris made a move and smiled at her weakly; Ivy nodded at her with fury. "Some big joke—my *'family'* . . . and my hustler boyfriend."

She pushed past Frank and slammed the door of her room.

Frank whirled on them. "You're all fired!"

"I don't need that crummy job," Tim said, sullenly turning his back.

"I don't mean from the job, cretin. I mean from the family. And *get a haircut!*"

"Don't you shout at him that way!" Doris put a protective arm around Tim's shoulders. Gena backed up cautiously to the telephone.

"You were in on it too!" Frank waved his glass at Doris, spilling part of his drink and an ice-cube on the floor.

"She just found out . . ." Gena offered in Doris's defense.

"And you stay off that phone!" Frank pointed at her, menacingly aimed at the phone.

"I have to cally Lenny . . ." she explained, whining unpleasantly.

"There's another cretin!"

"If you think I'm going to let him walk into this . . ." Frank moved deliberately toward her and Gena slowly hung up the receiver. He looked quite capable of tearing the wires from the wall.

Satisfied, he glanced at the melting ice-cube on the floor and waited until Gena edged back to Tim and Doris and they stood in a line facing him.

"Now," he said softly. "I want to know what you did to that girl"—he shouted at the top of his lungs—"who happens to be better than all of you put together!"

"Frank, will you calm down?"

He calmed down and slowly, prodding and threatening, shaking clenched fists and wheedling, he managed to get the story out of them. He paced the floor, his anger growing, his face getting redder—and they broke their line and told him, avoiding each other's faces, leaving nothing out.

Ivy stormed into her room and paced angrily to the bed, to the closet, stopped for a moment, to the bed again, hands clenched and moving with frustration until she came to rest in the middle of the room, breathing deeply and willed herself to stop trembling. She held her hands up to check, and moved purposefully into the bathroom and working cautiously she finished making-up. The face in the mirror looked strange to her—hard and tense, and yet oddly expressionless—and she moved a hand lightly up one cheek and pulled at the unfamiliar bangs on her forehead.

She blotted her lipstick carefully on a tissue and threw it under the sink, missing the wastebasket. It lay in a crumbled ball and she consciously, curiously, decided not to pick it up.

Make-up kit in hand, she paused to get a sweater from the dresser. With an angry scowl she picked up the little ashtray from the Japanese restaurant and hurled it against the wall. It broke cleanly into four pieces and fell silently on the rug.

Satisfied, she collected the things from her bed and headed for Eddie and the waiting limousine. She did not look back.

". . . . Then Jack Parks and Par-Tal are fired, too! You people are the *worst!*"

Frank broke off as Ivy burst into the kitchen, pushing past without a word, eyes straight ahead, walking purposefully for the front door.

"Ivy, I'll take you," he said.

She stopped; her voice was cool and controlled. "Thank you, Mr. Austin. But I . . . I have my limousine." She nodded, expressionless, at Doris and Gena and Tim.

The Austins watched after her in silence, listening to the car door slam and, a moment later to the crunch of the limousine moving down the gravel driveway.

Suddenly Doris broke the silence, moving wildly through the kitchen, opening drawers and slamming them shut.

"All right!" she yelled at them. "If that's the way you want it, that's the way it's going to be! I don't need *any* maids!" She came up with a long-handled utensil, a metal halfcircle full of holes at one end, and looked at it with distrust. "I ran this house before Ivy came, and I can do it again!" She suddenly whirled to face Frank who was looking at her open-mouthed. "So I *won't* go to Europe on the buying trip! So I *won't* work in the store anymore! Who cares!"

She smirked at him triumphantly and wrenched open the oven door. Looking around frantically, she located the potholder and pulled the roasting pan awkwardly toward her, jerking it forward too far over the front of the oven shelf. The pan teetered precariously and the steaming roast beef, as if starring in a silent-comedy sequence, slithered from the pan and skittered across the floor.

Doris watched it in shock, the color draining from her face; as the moisture welled up in her eyes she wailed, burst into tears and ran out and up the stairs, slamming the bedroom door behind her.

Frozen in tableau, Tim and Gena stared at the roast on the floor, a spotty dark line of juices marking its slide like tire rubber on asphalt. Frank, shoulders slumped, walked to the sink and slowly poured out his drink, carefully directing it into the center of the drain.

He tried to remember the last time he had seen Doris cry; he couldn't. His anger melted away, and he looked at his children, at their bewildered faces, and carefully rinsed his glass and put it silently on the drain.

"Gena," he said gently. "Pick up that roast and dust it off." He touched Tim lightly on the shoulder and patted her arm. "Your mother and I are going to have a nice, little talk."

Frank walked evenly up the stairs as Gena hurriedly got a plate for the roast; Tim found a sponge to wet at the sink and worked on the linoleum.

The roast safely on the counter, the floor wiped clean, Gena and Tim sat at the breakfast table peering anxiously at the stairs, listening to the silence. Slowly Tim turned a stricken gaze at Gena—and then the door which had closed behind Ivy.

Chapter Thirteen

"No! And that's final, man." Jack took a cigarette from the box. He smiled lightly as he discarded the little wax match in the ashtray and sat down on the couch. "Don't even ask. I am *not* working on the truck tonight." He relaxed against the cushions and watched Billy pace the living room to marshal his wits for the assault.

"Okay," Billy said. "I *grant* you that it's tough— working both shifts. Especially since you had such a hard *time* last night. . . ." He put his hands in mock protest at the interruption that didn't come.

Jack crossed his ankles on the table and rested his head in the cup of his laced fingers. This is going to be good, he thought.

"I just thought you might like to know that not one"—he held up a finger and paused dramatically—"but *two* of the guys came down with the flu this afternoon." Billy smiled sweetly, cocking his head to one side.

Oh no! Jack groaned inaudibly, sat up and flicked his cigarette in the ashtray in disgust. Billy had him nailed.

"Which means, partner, that either you ride up front with Jerry tonight so the reserve dealer and me can work the tables . . . or we cancel out some reservations." He handed Jack the list. "Now, *who* on this list is going to like that? Is there a single visiting fireman among them? No? Just a full complement of regulars?" Billy was warming up to it now, gesturing broadly, posturing and using a full range of facial expressions to show just how reasonable he could be.

Jack handed him back the list and Billy started reading it from the top, hammering *away* at him. "Mrs. Brill? How about her? She only shows up about eight or nine times a month, after all. She wouldn't mind, I'm sure. . . . Or the twins? That's it! We'll cancel out those nice twin widow ladies." He looked up from the list and spread his arms. "We can *easily* make up what they would lose by working the shipping trucks for an extra week of Sundays. Or maybe——"

Jack shut him off with a hand, hunching forward to put out his cigarette. "Yeah. Sure. You are one *lucky* fellow." He grinned in spite of himself. "If you call taking advantage of someone *else* having the flu lucky."

Billy saluted him with the list. "Usual time."

"I've got a date with Ivy. Eddie took her home to pick up some things." He frowned.

"Well, isn't that terrible!" Billy said, sympathetically shaking his head, making little clucking noises. "How did that *nasty* kid get you to do it *this* time? Did he threaten to——"

"Cut it, man. You've got me on the truck—don't press your luck."

Billy looked at him thoughtfully. "Listen, Jack, this set-up is too good to louse it up by getting involved with——"

"Lay off!" he said, surprised at the strength of his annoyance.

Billy shook his head. "Okay. Okay." He walked to the door, brushing his mouth lightly with the knuckles of a hand. "Only . . ."

"Only what?"

Billy turned back to face him. "Only that every time *you* get hooked up with a respectable dame *I* end up in trouble. Why is that, Jack? Like how come the first night you bring her on the truck I forget to turn the key and get locked in the elevator for six hours?. That's never happened before. And it worries me. You know that, buddy, it *worries* me!"

And Jack had to admit it, laughing helplessly—Billy sure looked worried.

Ivy stormed across the lobby, the overnight case firmly gripped in her hand, her mouth set in a thin, determined line; she was ready. Ready for anything but Edna who entered the lobby almost simultaneously from the elevator with two of the radiophone girls; all three were wearing mini-dresses, looking chic and beautiful and obviously ready for their night off.

"Hi." Edna waved off the attendant who doffed his hat and walked past to the door with the girls. "We tried to call you, but the radio in Eddie's car doesn't seem to be working."

"Why were you calling?"

Edna shrugged. "Two of the dealers came down with the flu so Jack has to work tonight. They left about ten minutes ago."

"He's *gone?*" Her voice echoed, hollow in the space of the lobby.

Edna nodded. "They waited as long as they could. But you can still catch them at the warehouse. Eddie will drive you."

Ivy shook her head. "He left as soon as I got out." She looked down at the little overnight bag. I can't go back to the Austins, she thought. I just *can't.*

"How about a cab?" Edna suggested. She checked her watch. "They won't be leaving the warehouse for at least half an hour. It'll be close but you might get there in time. Want to give it a try?"

Ivy frowned, unable to decide.

"Well . . . what d'you say?" Edna made a slight move, obviously anxious to get going herself.

Ivy looked at the girls waiting at the door, talking easily with the attendant, sure of themselves. "Yes . . . thank you," she said. "That sounds like a good idea."

"Fine." She called to him. "Get Miss Moore a cab, please. She's in a hurry."

Ivy watched Edna and her friends walk down the street, heads high, backs straight, proud of themselves, unself-conscious in clothes she wouldn't even try *on* . . . and she envied their poise. They turned a corner and were out of sight by the time the attendant had whistled-up a cab. He helped her in, gave the address to the driver and closed her door firmly; he doffed his cap as they pulled away and Ivy settled back against the seat and refused to think about what she would do if the truck was gone.

By the time they reached the Queens Midtown Tunnel, she was chatting easily with the driver, her determination renewed, her fingers lightly tapping the top of the overnight case in a steady, rolling cadence.

"This the place?" The driver swiveled around in his seat to look at her. "Don't look like no place for a girl to be going alone at night."

The truck was backed against the platform with no

one yet in the cab; the warehouse looked dark and deserted.

"It's okay," she said. "I . . . work here." She handed him a bill and waited for her change. "Actually there are quite a few people working tonight. Inventory, you know."

"But there aren't any lights, lady. This ain't no place to get stranded."

"No windows," she said. "Thanks, but there's no need to worry." She gave him a good tip and opened her door just as Eddie drove Jack's convertible out of the warehouse.

The driver looked relieved; his tires squealed as he drove off.

The overnight case swinging at her side, Ivy headed for the warehouse door, her anger returning, growing stronger with each step as the gravel became more and more uncomfortable against the poor protection of her thin shoe soles.

She stopped at the door, glanced around, then headed for Jerry who was the only person in sight; he was closing the latch on the back of the truck and he looked up quickly at the sound of her heels on the concrete floor Then Jack, scowling in reaction to the unknown footsteps, appeared from behind the far side of the truck, zipping up his coveralls.

She broke her stride and weakened momentarily as he stopped short, a smile growing from the corners of his mouth in obvious pleasure at the sight of her.

Clenching her free hand, admonishing herself to be firm, she planted her feet to let him know that she was angry.

He crossed the space between them with long, easy strides. "Hi! Listen, we tried to call. I thought I could get off tonight, but——"

"Two of the dealers have the flu . . . I know."

He nodded in agreement. "And we only have one reserve dealer so I was stuck."

"I want to talk to you." Her voice was flat, the tone icy and tough.

"'Is something wrong?" He cocked his head, curious when she shook off his attempt to take her arm. "Can't we talk on the truck?" he asked.

"What I've got to say won't keep."

Jerry called to them from the door, heading for the cab; he pointed to his watch and waited, obviously impatient.

Ivy stood her ground, refusing to budge.

"We're getting a late start as it is," Jack said. "Are you sure it can't wait?"

She answered him by remaining silent, by not so much as blinking.

"Okay," he called out to Jerry: "Start up. I'll be with you in a minute." He acknowledged Jerry's nod with a wave of his hand, took the overnight case and, getting a firm grip on her arm, steered them slowly for the door.

"Let's see now," he said lightly. "You left me about

. . . three hours ago?"

She turned her face away from his.

"Three hours ago," he said, holding up the watch strapped to his wrist for her to see, the overnight case turned awkwardly out from his bent wrist. "And three hours ago everything was fine."

They left the warehouse and Jack let go of her to close and lock the door, testing the knob unnecessarily. He took her arm again and half turned her toward him in the dim light from the bulb over the door, but she offered only her profile.

"Now you show up on the warpath. So answer one little question. What happened in the meantime?" He let go of her and leaned back against the warehouse door, waiting.

And she turned now to face him, her eyes blazing, her back suddenly stiff and unyielding. "I found out why you took me out."

He frowned. "I see. . . ."

"Now *you* answer one little question." She glared at him. "If it'd just been a question of staying in good with the Austins, would you have asked me?"

He thought it over carefully, not avoiding her eyes weighing it all up, taking his time. "Probably not," he said finally, giving himself some room to maneuver.

"In that case"—she folded her arms and drew them tight against her midriff—"I want a job."

"What!" He straightened up, shifting the overnight case to his other hand.

"I need a job. I quit the Austins tonight. Besides," she continued, getting warmed up and feeling mean, "isn't that what you do with all the chicks you discard . . give them jobs?"

Jack decided to get her angry more often—her eyes were flashing and he liked the way she looked, he fought down a smile.

"I thought you didn't want anything from any guy," he said in a serious voice, teasing her.

"That's until now! I never met one like you before. You are really terrible."

He grinned in spite of himself.

Ivy stamped her foot in anger, glancing down in fury as the gravel hurt her foot. She looked at him and sputtered, "You should be *ashamed* of yourself, you . . . you . . . *West Indian!*"

He was only partially successful in fighting back his chuckle, but the sound he made was covered by Jerry who suddenly honked the truck's horn in an impatient cadence. Jack took Ivy's arm and hustled her to the truck, opening the door and urging her in.

"What're you doing?" she asked, furious, resisting him.

He pushed her up with both hands, the handle of the overnight bag hard against her back. "We've got a date, haven't we? *In.*"

She moved reluctantly, nodded at Jerry and pushed back tight against the seat, folding her arms in front of her, her hands clenched in tight fists. She refused to look at Jack who climbed in beside her, slamming the door.

Jerry glanced at them thoughtfully, started to say something but thought better of it and slowly moved the truck away from the loading platform.

Jack swung the overnight case into the space behind the seat; it brushed against Ivy's arm.

"On top of everything else, you're probably also a murderer!" She glared at him, her hand clutching the grazed spot.

He carefully removed the protective hand and stroked her arm comfortingly as if she were an injured child. He was grinning easily now and Ivy began to lose her bravado, pulling away from him reluctantly.

"Well, just as long as you know it's not *my* fault Mr. Austin found out everything and isn't going to use Par-Tal anymore." She flounced back against the seat, careful to avoid touching him.

"*Wonderful!*" Jerry looked over at Jack, leaning forward to peer around Ivy, his eyebrows forming small ridges between his eyes, his mouth tight against his lips. "Now we've lost the Austin account because of her."

"Because of *him!*" Ivy said indignantly, poking Jack in the ribs with her elbow.

"Sure. . . ." He glanced away from her in disgust.

"Jerry, just drive!" Jack's voice left no room for argument.

"I'm *driving!*" He threw his hands in the air,

bounced off the back seat and quickly reclaimed the wheel of the moving truck.

Jack caught Ivy's prodding arm by the wrist, straightening it out to lock it safely against his side with his upper arm, examining her fingers with both his hands, opening and closing them, playing with her hand. He resisted her attempt to pull away with an increase in pressure of his arm muscles, and a light slap on the back of her hand. He smiled and slowly shook his head; she made a face at him and stared out the front windshield.

Jerry flipped the directional signal; Jack took Ivy's wrist tightly in his left hand.

"Turn right," he said.

"We're going to Jersey," Jerry said. "To go to Jersey we go to the Lincoln Tunnel, which is *left*."

"That's right. Turn right. We're going out Northern Boulevard."

"Into Nassau *again!*" Jerry jerked the truck to a stop at the corner.

Jack braced himself and caught the free arm Ivy swung at him: "I'm *not* going back there!"

"You *are* going back there," he said, straining a little to hold her, surprised at her strength.

Jerry looked at them, took a deep breath and exhaled noisily. "Jack," he said. "You're *crazy!*"

Jack looked at him, pushing Ivy back against the seat. "*Jerry!*" he said menacingly as if it was obvious he didn't need any more problems.

"Okay!" Jerry shifted the truck noisily and slowly grinded his way right.

Ivy stopped struggling and Jack gingerly tested her, slightly relaxing the pressure on one wrist. So far so good, he thought, letting the hand go altogether. She pulled it away and he smiled, just a bit too soon: Ivy pulled her other arm free and took a healthy swing at him. He laughed aloud and caught her before she did any damage.

Jerry snorted and headed reluctantly toward King's Point.

The roast was surprisingly good, much to everyone's relief, and Gena and Tim fussed about it embarrassingly.

Frank listened to them, annoyed, sipping his drink, determined to get through the rest of the evening without another scene. He glanced over at Doris: her color was coming back and her eyes had cleared. The dinner was restoring her confidence. He helped himself to another piece of meat and on an impulse carved off the other seasoned end slice, Tim's favorite, and passed it to him. He refused his son's surprised look of thanks and directed his attention to his plate.

Gena stayed in the kitchen to help Doris without being asked and Tim followed Frank into the living room. He accepted a small brandy and sipped it slowly, sitting silently on the couch, fidgeting with his hair, smoking a cigarette.

Frank plopped into the easy chair, his stomach full, and carefully ministered to the lighting of his Cuban cigar. He glanced at Tim and searched about for something to say, staring at the new ash on his cigar thoughtfully. Tim put out his cigarette, deliberately lining it up with the ashtray to crush it without bending the butt and got up restlessly; he headed for the patio. Frank followed him with his eyes; he wished he had a newspaper.

By the time Doris and Gena were done in the kitchen Frank had finished his third brandy and Tim had escaped to the solitude of the pool house; they had exchanged goodnights.

"That was a good dinner, Doris," Frank said. "I really enjoyed it."

"Thank you, dear. It was all right, wasn't it?" She sat down on the couch and began worrying a hangnail that had developed while washing the dishes.

Gena switched on the radio, fretting with the dial until she was satisfied. Then she stood in the draft from the patio, rocking with the music, annoyed that Lenny wasn't coming over after all.

Frank poured himself another drink, stared at the speaker in irritation and switched off the radio. He looked over at Doris; she sat with her eyes closed, her head leaning against the back of the sofa.

"I'm going to bed," she announced suddenly. "I have a *terrible* headache."

"Well, that's a good idea, then," Frank said. "I'll be

up in a while." He carried the glass and bottle with him to the couch and placed them within easy reach.

"Me, too." Gena followed her mother up the stairs to her own bedroom, heading for the phone.

Frank stared at the empty steps for a long time. He drained his glass and refilled it from the bottle.

Billy had an awful feeling, a premonition, and he was on edge. Aside from which the blackjack table was losing money. It had been losing money ever since he had taken over the deal—just as had happened at the roulette wheel and at the craps table before that. And now he had just dealt out not one, but *two* blackjacks at a table of five players. He looked at them and paid the winners. *Black Jacks*. Without thinking he swung his head toward the cab of the truck.

On the other side of the panel, protected from Billy's view, Jerry was driving the truck down a peaceful residential road. He was obviously nervous and his eyes shifted frequently from the road ahead of him to the side mirror.

Ivy sat quietly for the most part, only occasionally attempting to free her right wrist from Jack's grip.

"Turn right."

Jerry turned right; he had gone about a mile down the road when Jack signalled him.

"That's it to the right there. Pull up past the driveway."

Jerry slowed the truck to a stop, knowing better than to argue.

Ivy pulled back against the seat and braced her feet on the floor. "I'm *not* going into that house with you."

Jack ignored her and opened the door.

"I'll have Eddie pick you up," Jerry said.

"I won't be long. Just circle around awhile."

"Oh, man! . . ." Circle around in Nassau! On restricted back roads! Jerry leaned his head against the arms he braced out straight on the steering wheel. He didn't know whether to laugh or cry.

Without looking up he listened to Jack pull Ivy down from the cab, coming back for the case behind the seat. Her feet dragged on the driveway.

"C'mon!" he heard Jack say.

"I'll just lock myself in my room!"

God, Jerry thought. Why hadn't she done that last night!

He reached for the buzzing phone, talking before it reached his ear. "Yes, Billy."

Billy looked around the casino—no one else seemed to notice that they weren't traveling. He cupped his hand over the phone.

"Hey, man. Why are we stopped?"

"You're not going to like it," Jerry said, bracing for the explosion. "Jack's got us stopped outside that dame's house. In Nassau."

"Where?" Billly didn't believe him; he had to be kidding.

"Well, to be exact, we're stopped on *the* road through *the* residential section of King's Point."

"You're *insane!*" Billy sank back against the wall and signaled Norma for a drink.

"Jack, man. *He* gave the order," Jerry protested.

"Then *he's* insane. Get out of here, man." Billy paced in front of the phone, taking short, nervous steps, the phone held tightly in both hands, listening to Jerry explain. "All right, then," he said nervously. "Give him ten minutes. But call Eddie to pick him up anyway!"

"Okay."

"And *move* it." He started to hang up but pulled the phone back to his mouth. "*Insane!*" He slammed the phone on its hook, walked to Norma who was holding up a drink for him and downed it in two swallows.

He headed to the bar for a refill. *Respectable chicks*, he thought, pouring himself a double.

"Billy, they're getting impatient." Norma pointed to the twenty-one table.

He nodded and headed over, carrying his drink with him, apologizing for the delay. Shuffling professionally, he passed the cards for a cut and dealt out the hands.

A loud yelp of pleasure rose from the table: Billy stared. I don't know why I'm surprised, he thought suddenly. After all, it figured: at the table of five there were not two . . . but three blackjacks.

Tim was lying on the couch blowing small, even, smoke rings and lazily breaking them with his cigarette. Janis Ian's mournful voice sang softly from the speaker behind his head. He scratched irritably at a mosquito bite just under the waistband of his khakis. The yellow insect bulb over the front door of the pool house cast a pale, indistinct light through the window; the red 'on' indicator of the stereo amplifier was a bright magnet for his eyes.

He was thinking it over again, checking the plan out, deciding how he would put it into words, when the sound of a—*was* it a truck? he wondered—truck seemed to approach the driveway of the house, only to disappear. He jabbed his cigarette in the ashtray and stared out the window: Jack Parks was dragging Ivy up the driveway, pulling her by the arm, heading for the front of the house. The truck's motor started up, the sound almost deafening in the still night air.

Tim left the pool house in a run and cut across the grass to the kitchen door; he was already in the hall when Frank stumbled to answer the doorbell, a drink in his hand. Doris and Gena appeared at the top of the steps and walked down to stand behind Tim; they waited silently for Frank to reach the door.

Ivy tensed as she heard the footsteps in the hall; the front-door light clicked on. She made her move as the door began to open, pulling away from Jack and pushing through, making a break for the refuge of the kitchen—but her way was blocked by the family in the hall and Jack caught her without any trouble.

"Now, just take it easy," he said, holding on to prevent her from escaping again.

The silence in the hall was a ringing, almost palpable sensation.

Frank still held the door open, staring at them, openmouthed, vaguely bleary-eyed, disbelief evident as he looked first at Ivy and then at Jack. Then he moved, shocking their tableau into action: he slammed the door.

"Doris, call the police!" He swung his drink-holding arm toward her and headed for the living room; Ivy automatically reached for the ice cube that splashed out of the glass.

Jack frowned and tugged her arm. "Mr. Austin. Just a minute."

Frank stopped in the middle of the room and whirled on them. "On top of everything else"—he shouted at Jack—"on top of everything else I guess we can add a kidnaping charge!" He looked at his wife and Gena, who had moved to his side, for confirmation; Tim was standing next to Ivy, and Frank included his son in his eyes' sweep of the enemy camp.

"Sorry, sir," Jack replied. "I'm not stealing her away. I'm bringing her *back*."

"But she obviously doesn't *want* to come back." Frank waved his drink at Jack's hand on Ivy's wrist.

"That's right!" Ivy glared and tried unsuccessfully to pull her wrist free. Tim made a move toward her but abruptly stopped; instead he helped himself to a drink and walked the bottle to his father who signalled him violently for a refresher.

"Frank . . ." Unable to prevent Tim from pouring the drink, worried, Doris plucked ineffectually at Frank's sleeve.

"*I'm* handling this." He shrugged her off irritably. "Why haven't the police arrived?"

"Mr. Austin . . ." Jack's voice sounded strangely calm and controlled in the tension-filled room.

"Have I mentioned we're through with Par-Tal?" Frank rocked back on his heels and gestured with his glass. Ivy looked at the spot of dampness as he splashed liquor on the rug; it's going to leave a stain, she thought.

"Par-Tal has nothing to do with this," Jack said.

Frank shrugged; it didn't matter one way or the other. "My lawyer will send a cancellation letter in the morning."

Frank seemed to calm down a little and Doris, relieved, sat down gratefully; her headache had returned. She got an unpleasant, guilty twinge of satisfaction knowing that Frank was going to feel worse in the morning. Gena made herself inconspicuous in the corner chair, tucking her feet up, the perfect spectator.

Frank unconsciously ran a hand through his thinning hair in a perfect imitation of Tim. He stared at the drink in his hand, swirled it to hear the ice clink against the glass, then he studied Jack thoughtfully before downing the drink.

He placed the glass carefully on the table. "A few days ago we were a normal, alienated, American family." Frank looked at his wife, his daughter; he glared at his son. "The minute we started talking to one another," he said to Jack, looking for an explanation, "the whole thing came apart."

"That would seem to be your problem."

"But it's your *fault!*" He raised his voice and walked close to them, pointing straight at Jack. "You're the only new element added to the situation."

Jack shook his head violently and held Ivy's hand up to move her forward. "Wrong!" he said. "It all came apart when Ivy said she was quitting."

Frank weaved a bit, the liquor catching up to him, and Jack let Ivy reach out to steady him and to guide him to the couch where no one else moved to help him. Ivy picked up his glass to take it to the kitchen but her respite was over; Jack took the glass from her, put it back on the table noisily, and took her hand in his.

"Are you all that helpless you can't live without one little colored girl?" His voice was quiet, directed at all of them, and Jack's question hung in the air, an invisible force that seemed to galvanize the Austins into proving they could move: Doris got up and went to sit at her husband's side; Frank leaned awkwardly forward and retied both his shoelaces, Gena, who had been totally silent, came to claim the chair Doris had just left; and Tim lit a cigarette and joined his parents on the couch.

Ivy was fidgeting at Jack's side, uncomfortable and painfully aware of the tension in the room, of distances among the Austins who sat and watched Jack now, waiting for him to tell them the answer, unable to even look at each other.

And then Frank slowly shook his head, his anger draining away; he seemed to sober up all at once as his reason returned. He looked at Jack thoughtfully. "It just so happens she held this house together."

Doris pulled at him. "Frank, that's not true!" she said, her voice the indignant whine of one unwilling to acknowledge a painful fact.

"Isn't it?" he said quietly. "I think you'd better give it a little thought, Doris." Frank watched her grow silent, toy with her earring, unable to meet his eyes. "That goes for you, too, Gena . . . *and* for you, Tim." He looked at each of his children for a long moment before turning back to Jack. "Why'd you bring her back?" Frank got up and walked to them.

"I guess . . ." Jack thought it over comfortably. "Because nine years do count for something. It shouldn't end this way," he said. "Not because of me, anyway. If Ivy leaves——" he broke off and corrected himself. "*When* Ivy leaves, it should be done the proper way."

"And I suppose you're not interested in saving the account?"

"No," Jack said firmly. "Not on your terms, man. I've done a good job for you for six years, and if that doesn't count for anything, well. . ." He shrugged. "There are other accounts."

Frank locked his hands behind him, looking at Jack thoughtfully, his head cocked slightly to one side; he nodded his agreement and held out his hand. Jack was pleased with the firmness of the handshake.

"Now," he said to Ivy quietly, "why don't you give these people a nice, proper two-weeks' notice, and in two weeks we'll talk about a job. . . ." He lifted her eyes up to his with a hand under her chin. He could feel the pain in her eyes; it was a knot in his stomach. "Or anything else you want to talk about." He dropped his hand.

She didn't lower her eyes. "You mean that?"

"Sure I mean that." Yes, I mean that, he thought.

"Wait a minute, man . . ." Tim jumped from the couch, running a hand through the hair on his forehead, animated and nervous.

Jack's voice was angry: "As for you, the next time you're looking for somebody to serve your miserable needs——"

"That's not what it's about, man," he said, so seriously that Jack's anger was gone before he could hold on to it.

He looked at him curiously. "Then, what, man?"

"It came to me today while I was shooting baskets." He broke off for a minute, then straightened his back and continued in a rush. "It all fell into place when you drove up in the limousine, Ive . . ." He reached out and took her hand. "The thing is, Ive . . . I think we should get married."

They stared at him: Frank and Doris, Gena, Jack and Ivy. The silence was deafening.

"Or, if that seems like too big a move for openers," he said quickly, "we live together for a time. Get a little place in the East Village."

"Tim!" Ivy wailed.

"Okay, the West Village."

"He means it, Mom," Gena said. Doris nodded at her in shock.

"Ive, it makes perfect sense to me." Tim had let go of her hand and was moving now, making short little steps in front of her, his arms gesturing expressively close to his chest. "You're very attractive and you cook great . . . and no one can say we don't know each other."

This is one incredible kid, Jack thought, looking at his tangled hair and dirty clothes. The look of hope on his face was so touching that Jack moved slowly to the chair in the corner and sat down.

"Ive, there's only one problem as far as I can see," Tim said.

"And what . . ." Frank cleared his throat noisily. "And what might . . . that be?" he asked his son.

"Well," Tim shuffled his feet. "Dad . . . you and Mom might object to the fact that she's six years older than I am."

Ivy turned away from him. "Five-and-a-half . . ." She glanced over at Jack and he was blurred from the moisture beginning to well up in her eyes.

Tim moved very close to her and spoke so softly that Jack strained to hear him. "If *you* asked me to, Ive, I'd get a haircut, and wear shoes, and even get a square job." He looked for a reaction. "Like in advertising," he said hopefully.

And, unable to control her tears, Ivy fled from him, through the dining room into the kitchen, disappearing around the bend toward her own door.

"Think it over, Ive!" Tim called after her. He looked self-consciously around the room and sat down on the ottoman, his shoulders hunched, his arms falling toward the floor between his legs. "I guess she has to think it over," he said, raising a hand to clear off his forehead.

Frank looked at his son for a long time; slowly an expression of understanding softened his face. "Maybe . . . maybe you shouldn't get a haircut," he said.

Jack headed for the front door, stopping momentarily in the hallway to look at the Austins in the living room. He could see the subtle change that had taken place, feel a release of tension and a re-found—family unity?— He wasn't sure. But whatever it was, it was good—too good to interrupt even to say that he was leaving.

Chapter Fourteen

Billy could never remember the action being so
noisy; the flap of cards being shuffled, the clatter of
the little ball in the spinning roulette wheel, the jan-
gle of chips, even the faint *whish* of the baccarat
cards being slipped from the shoe—they all merged
and found the tender spot above and behind his right
eye, as if magnified and heightened and carried uner-
ringly on a laser beam.

Billy had moved to work the roulette wheel, hoping
for a break in his luck, and in the half dozen spins
since the truck had started up again he had paid off
on twenty-two winning number bets in addition to
the less expensive color bets. It was unbelievable—ab-
solutely unbelievable. He felt a deep sympathy for

Dr. Morgan, the only bettor who had not won at all—he was also the only one at the table who owed markers. That figures too, Billy thought ruefully. With a worried frown he called for all bets and, hesitating slightly, he turned the wheel for the seventh time, watched the little ball skilfully avoid the double zero: there were three large bets on the seven and this time even the chiropractor had red: he pulled in the few losing chips, counted out the payoffs and signalled Harry that he was digging into the reserve chips.

Harry slowly made the necessary note in the receipt book, surprised: it was a first, the first time Billy had needed his reserve, and he thought a minute about the consequences. It was his policy to dock a dealer one of his nights off for hitting the reserves; two nights if the table went broke. It happened occasionally, not often. How do I dock the boss, Harry wondered. Maybe I lock him *out* for a night.

Billy recouped a bit on the next spin and looked around quickly as he sensed the truck slowing down; he checked his watch: they had been moving for exactly ten minutes. He called a two-minute break and headed for the phone.

"Jerry, what's happening?"

"We're stopped. Eddie's not here yet—said it'd take him at least another fifteen minutes."

"Cut it, man—you know what I mean!"

"He's nowhere in sight," Jerry said flatly.

"Figures, doesn't it? What the hell is he *doing?*"

Billy waved off Harry's warning glance but he lowered his voice. "How's the traffic? Any . . . any you-know-what's around?" The thought was very unpleasant.

"So far, so good." Jerry looked anxiously toward the house. "No red lights . . . nothing that looked like an unmarked car, either. Mostly station wagons and Cadillacs and a few Mercedes and Lincolns." He tensed as headlights cut the dark, heading for the truck; a gaggle of noisy teenagers packed in an open convertible looked at the truck curiously but drove by without slowing down.

"Okay. Stay put, until I tell you." Billy slammed down the phone and noted with disgust that his hands were shaking; he signalled wildly for Harry. Jack's the only one, he thought. He is the *only* one who can do this to me. He's the only one who *does* do this to me. Why do I put up with it? *Why?*

"Harry, I've got to get off the table. What can we do?"

"What's up?"

Billy clenched his fists, fighting to keep a semblance of control. "Don't ask," he said. "Don't *ask*. Just figure some way to get me *off!*"

Harry looked around the truck thoughtfully. "Well . . . I *suppose* we could divide up one of the twenty-one tables . . . but there may be some objections. . . ."

202

"Too bad. Do it. I'm going up front." He headed for the panel.

Jerry jumped at the unexpected sound of the panel opening, and looked at Billy's dinner jacket in dismay.

"Your coveralls, man. Where are they?"

"Forget it . . . *where is he?*" Billy's voice was shrill and loud.

"*You've* got eyes—he's nowhere in *sight*." He could feel Billy's tension amplify his own and he banged the heels of his hands on the steering wheel. "*Coveralls,*" he hissed. "It's your *own* rule: coveralls over any dinner jackets in the cab. If we get stopped we've got at least a *chance* if we're in coveralls. If you don't have yours, use Jack's—it's right behind the seat. *Please . . . !*"

"Coveralls?" Billy asked, his voice strangely controlled. "*Jack's* coveralls. You want me to put on *his. . . .*" He broke off and suddenly began to shake. "Why the hell isn't *Jack* in Jack's coveralls? Answer me *that.* Answer me *that,* will you? Answer me *that.*"

Jerry leaned back and slumped down in the seat, as if to hide from the piercing voice that yelled at him.

"And where *is* he? Tell me *that,* will you? Answer me *that!* No? You don't know?" He leaned close to Jerry and tugged on his sleeve. "*I'll* tell you," he said, his words unnaturally drawn out, his fingers plucking hard at Jerry's arm. "He's in there plotting against me. That's *not* what he *thinks* he's doing. But that's what he's *doing.*" Billy looked at the fabric in his fingers as if

203

he'd never seen it before, rubbed it between his fingers and started to shake again.

"*And you want me to put on his coveralls,*" he screamed. Billy's mouth stayed open, working at words that would not come.

Jack listened to the truck slow to a stop, the idling motor a disturbing sound, out-of-place among the usual night sounds of King's Point. He was standing in the hall, within arm's reach of the front door knob, trying to make up his mind. He could hear a few isolated words of the Austins' hesitant attempts at conversation in the living room; the rumble of the truck made it difficult to identify the voices.

He took a half-step forward, stopped and made a deliberate about-face. Purposefully, not hurrying but without hesitation, he traced Ivy's path and knocked on the door that was obviously her room.

"It's open, Tim."

She was hastily drying her eyes on a handkerchief, sitting on the bed in the neat, sterile room, and she turned away when she saw Jack. He closed the door carefully and sat down next to her on the bed.

"Listen!" Jack turned her around to face him.

"How am I going to tell him no?" Ivy said softly. She played with the handkerchief, wringing it into a tight roll and crushing it into a ball.

"He'll understand," Jack said. "The age difference . . ."

"It's not funny." She looked very serious.

"I guess it isn't," he agreed, remembering the look on Tim's face. She's really very fond of him, Jack thought.

He pushed away a curl of hair that had fallen out of place to cover Ivy's ear. "At least you've been asked," he said lightly.

"It's the first time."

"Who knows . . . you play your cards right, and you might be asked again." The first time!

She got up suddenly and went to close a drawer that was open a fraction of an inch; she put her hands palm down on the top of the dresser, resting her weight hard against them.

"Why are you making me stay here?"

"No," Jack said. "I'm not making you do anything. But I'll tell you what I think you *ought* to do."

"What's that?" Her voice was stronger now, but she didn't turn around.

"It's still your night off, isn't it?" he asked.

She nodded her head.

"And you've been carrying that silly little suitcase around all night?"

She nodded again and he noticed the white ashtray pieces still laying on the floor. He picked one of them up and looked at it thoughtfully, tossing it back to the floor.

"And we *did* have a date. . . ." He stood at her side, not touching her, waiting.

205

"But I don't want to be like those other girls. . . . The ones you threw away."

And now he ran a finger lightly down her arm. "No chance," he said. No chance.

"Ivy, is Mr. Parks with you?" Gena's voice followed a loud knock on the door; Jack went to open it.

"Yes?"

"There's a hysterical man at the kitchen door who wants to see you." She pointed behind her.

"Tell him to go away." He followed the line of her point but the door was blocked from view.

Gena looked doubtful. "He's *very* hysterical."

"Okay," he said. "Tell him I'll be right there."

Ivy had moved back to the bed, watching him now, her eyes dry; he noticed that the handkerchief had disappeared, and that she had disposed of the broken ashtray, too.

"You come on out when you're ready." He thought she nodded slightly, but he couldn't be sure.

Billy, like a man possessed, waited for him at the top of the kitchen stairs; the sight of Jack sent him bounding to the driveway, arms flailing, feet kicking up gravel.

"Just like Kyoto!" he screamed, shaking a clenched fist. "*Just like Kyoto!*"

". . . What?" Gena had been right, he thought . . . *very* hysterical.

"That time we had leave. . . . You were supposed to meet me in the bar. . . ." Billy broke off and ran halfway to the truck that was parked across the top of the driveway. "Seven hours I waited, baby," he yelled, turning back, approaching in a broken-field running pattern. "Seven hours . . . then got into the fight with the two sailors and ended in *jail*. . . ."

"Man, are you crazy?"

"*Crazy!*" he yelled, crouching down only to spring back up. "Was I crazy that time I went from 'Frisco all the way to L. A. because you called me, and when I got there you'd gone off to Tijuana . . . ?"

"Billy . . ."

He held up a hand to shut Jack off and jabbed at his shoulder with a fist: "And two years ago, at Christmas, our *busiest* time, *you* disappeared to Pureto Rico. . . ."

Jack moved. "Man, will you come down!"

"It's *always broads!*" Billy yelled. "And I'm getting sick of it, baby. I've given you your last chance." He rocked back on his heels, waiting.

"Last chance at what?"

"At keeping your mind on business, *that's* what, man," Billy said, yelling his impatience. "Keeping your mind on *business*."

"Par-Tal's my business. You got any complaints?" He was getting angry himself and joined Billy on the path.

"And what do you call *that?*" Billy gestured wildly at the truck, waving with both arms. "A taxi service for lonely domestics?"

"You've flipped out, man!" Jack looked at him with disgust, his voice becoming as shrill as Billy's.

Billy shook his head violently, but he seemed to suddenly gain control, his movements grew less animated, his voice lost the edge of its shrillness.

"I'm telling you, man, I am bored with this behavior."

"And I'm bored with working nights on that *stupid truck*," Jack yelled, shaking his fist at the casino on wheels.

"And *I'm* bored with that square, daytime jive. Balancing books, making deliveries, making up to people like . . . these *Austins*." He counted it off on his fingers, planted his feet firmly and shook his head in emphasis. "You're going to put me *away* with all that, man!"

"What do you intend doing about it?" Jack wanted to know, his hands balled hard into his sides.

"You like Par-Tal? . . . You want Par-Tal? . . . You can *have* Par-Tal!"

"I'll take it," Jack said without hesitation.

"You got it!" Billy's voice was excited. "Just let me have the nighttime deal. We divvy right down the line. You get Par-Tal, I get that truck."

"That's a deal, man," Jack said immediately.

"You bet it's a deal, baby!"

"Shake!" Jack said, offering his hand.

They shook hands furiously, gripping hard, pumping their arms hard, finally slowing down and looking at each other curiously, drawing back a little, the anger gone and reason coming back to take over.

"You really mean that, Billy?" Jack asked cautiously.

"Sure I mean it," he said mildly, standing quiet now. "I guess the lawyers can work it out fair and square."

They paused in the night dimness and suddenly grinned at one another with their easy comraderie restored.

"Why didn't we think of that before?" Jack asked.

"I don't know." Billy shook his head slowly. "But it really makes sense, doesn't it? We each get what we want."

They were thinking it over, silent, adding it up, both of them pleased; a car pulled in from the road, cutting around in front of the truck, it's lights piercing the darkness. It stopped in the driveway; the motor cut out and the lights disappeared.

"That's Eddie with your car," Billy said. "I'll take him in the truck with me. He can ride shotgun for Jerry." He waved and started off down the driveway. "See you around, man."

Jack watched him reach the truck, become framed in the cab's light which flicked on when he opened the truck door and he suddenly hurried after him.

"Billy. . . . Listen, about Kyoto. . . ."

He turned around to face Jack.

"I *did* bail you out." It was necessary to remind him.

"Yeah . . ." he agreed, laughing.

Jack stood there, near the truck, and watched as Billy collected the driver. Eddie tossed the car keys to Jack, and settled into the cab with Jerry, as Billy disappeared through the panel into the back of the truck. The engine revved up, Jerry ground the gears, the big headlights split the peace of the road and laboriously the truck headed off into the night. Jack watched the red taillights disappear from view before tossing the car keys in his hand and heading for the convertible.

Ivy stood framed in the light of the front door, watching him; he stopped to look at her, at the little overnight bag in her hand. It's all falling into place, he thought.

Elated, he broke into a half-run, took the case from her and hustled her to the car.

"Now we are going to find out where the action is really *at*," he said happily. "I am a free man, baby, *free*." He pulled her against him briefly, hugging her close.

As Ivy slipped onto the seat of the car Gena walked a few steps out the front door with Tim behind her, watching them silently. Ivy acknowledged them with a little wave, and waved again when Jack started up the car and Frank and Doris also appeared in the doorway.

At the driveway's end Ivy looked back at the family group on the front steps; as Jack turned onto the main road, they were cut off from view. She stared down at her hands.

"Don't look so sad," Jack said. "You'll be back."

Ivy nodded. "But this is really like leaving. They believe it now."

"It's what you wanted, isn't it?" And I have what I want, he thought. Contentment: So this is what it feels like.

Ivy nodded slowly and looked at him. "But you may be making a bad mistake," she said seriously.

"What do you mean?"

"I could turn out to be an awful pain . . . because I'll want to do a lot of things for you."

He grinned and looked at her with pleasure.

". . . Like pick out your ties and press your shirts . . . and change your life." She was watching him, her eyes big, her body slightly tense, a nervous look to the corners of her mouth.

"Mmm-hm," he said, frowning at her. And he slowly put an arm around her shoulders and pulled her close to him, tight against his side.

"Doesn't that worry you?" Her voice was weak, muffled against his shoulder, her fingers played lightly with the lace front of his shirt.

". . . Yeah," he said solemnly. "It worries me."

"Oh." She made a slight move of withdrawal but he kept her from moving away.

"Like . . . how am I going to tell my nice laundry-man?" he asked. "Now *that's* something to worry about."

He slowed the car to a stop under a big tree, where the shoulder of the road widened a bit, and got out. Her puzzled look changed to a soft smile when he returned, holding out a leaf for her. She rubbed it between her fingers and smelled the freshness of it and he let her be for a moment before pulling her soft body hard against him, his hands working on her back, his mouth claiming hers greedily. . . .

The distant wail of police sirens shattered the stillness of a night and Jack stiffened, slowly untangling himself from her arms; she put a hand gingerly on his arm and cocked her head curiously as he frowned and slowly pulled the car back on to the road.

"Boy, am I glad to see you back," Harry said. "We have some mighty unhappy people in this here truck." He pointed to a pair of tall, heavy-set men wearing cowboy hats playing at the hastily enlarged twenty-one table near the bar. "They've calmed down a bit, but I really thought there was going to be trouble."

"I'll take care of them." Harry looked at Billy strangely.

"What happened, man? You sound like the cat that got the whole canary population."

"Tell you later." He weaved through the truck and made profuse apologies to the gamblers that had been displaced and in a very short time the tables had been put back in order. Billy took back the roulette wheel.

In the space of five minutes his mood sobered. It should *change*, he thought. I don't believe it. The relief dealer had recouped almost all that he had lost to the gamblers before he left the truck, but now Billy was signalling Harry that he again was dipping into the reserves. Soberly he handed Dr. Morgan back his last marker in payment for a winning bet, looking at the slip of paper with a frown. It doesn't add up. It just doesn't add up at all.

Jerry heard the wail of a police siren and looked hastily into the side mirror. He couldn't see the car and he relaxed slowly as the siren suddenly faded out.

"Five miles," he said to Eddie. "Five miles and we're back on the highway and this is going to be one hell of a long five-mile ride."

Eddie nodded in agreement. He had squirmed his way into Jack's coveralls, which were too big for him, and he was uncomfortably aware of the extra fabric bunched up against the small of his back.

They both watched in horror as the police car, red lights flashing, siren out, pulled up alongside and motioned them to a stop.

The cop was a burly, red-faced Irishman and he asked for Jerry's license and registration, looking at the truck curiously. "This road is restricted to trucks. Can't you read signs?"

"Sorry," Jerry said politely. "I missed a turn some-how, officer, and couldn't find my way back out. I flagged down a carful of kids and they said this was the best way to get where I'm headed."

The cop looked at the papers thoughtfully, checked out the license, and after what seemed like an eter-nity he nodded.

"I'll have to give you a ticket."

Jerry tried to look upset, which wasn't difficult. "Well, if you have to . . ."

And he stared in dismay at the dashboard phone, which rang loudly. He started to reach for it but the policeman slowly shook his head and motioned Jerry out of the cab, calling over to his partner. Jerry watched in horror as the cop slowly climbed up into the cab, keeping an eye on Eddie; he reached for the phone and held it to his ear.

"Okay, Jerry. Okay. Why the hell are we stopped this time?"

The officer looked at the phone, slowly hung it up again and motioned Eddie out of the cab. He left them, spread-eagled against the side of the truck after he searched them; his partner covered them with his gun and the Irishman headed for his patrol car. He called in reinforcements.

Billy looked at the phone in his hand: Jerry had hung up on him! He didn't believe it.

He signalled for Harry. "Jerry just hung up on me. And we're stopped. What do you think?"

Harry shook his head; he followed Billy's worried look at the panel.

The police sirens invaded, screaming even over the noise of the gambling; there wasn't even time to hide away the game receipts: the sirens moaned downwards to a stop, the inside of the truck went deadly silent. And as the police ax went to work on the outside lock, pandemonium took over. Billy calmly headed for the bar and threw down a straight double shot. He looked thoughtfully at the back door, straining against the blows aimed at it. And then they were open and the police floodlights hit them unmercifully.

Half of the patrons were already out of the truck when the phone buzzed. Harry quickly raised it to his ear, shrugging off the blue-coated arm that tried to take the phone.

"Yeah? . . . Where are *you!* . . . I'll try man. . . ." He looked around and spotted Billy at the bar.

"Billy . . . phone!"

"Not *now!*"

Harry could hardly hear him over the wails and screams of the almost totally hysterical women and the angry cries of the men.

"It's Jack," he yelled, yielding to the pressure of the cop pulling him toward the open back door.

Billy wended his way carefully to the back of the truck, trying to make himself inconspicuous; he picked up the phone.

"Yeah. . . ." He turned angrily to the cop who tried to pull him out. "Wait a minute, wait a minute! Can't you see I'm on the phone?"

The cop stopped and surprizingly decided to be reasonable.

"A fine mess you got me into, baby."

"But we're still partners, baby," Jack said. "And, like remember Kyoto . . . ? So I'll bail you out again."

The cop decided he had given him enough time, and reached again for Billy's arm. Billy fought desperately to keep the phone.

". . . And get to the lawyers right away. . . . No, what's the sense of you coming into this mess, too. Just call the lawyers!"

"Okay, will do. And Billy . . . looks like you'll have to work days with me again."

Billy looked at the phone in disgust, left it hanging free on its wire, and yielded to the now angry pressure the policeman applied to his arm. He maneuvered his way to the side of the truck and ended up leaning awkwardly against it, next to Jerry who had already been searched.

They glanced up in unison as Jack's car slowly drove by without stopping, and their eyes followed the car down the road.

"Respectable dames," Billy muttered. "It never fails."

Jerry turned his eyes reluctantly from the taillights of Jack's car and looked at Billy thoughtfully.

"I see what you mean," he said.

The sound of their forced, desperate laughter was so unusual that even Mrs. Brill stopped her hysterical protests and stared at them.

They saw the opened truck and the red flashing lights of the police cars as they rounded a turn in the road; Jack drove slowly by the well-lit concentrated area of action—the policemen with their drawn guns, the noise of the angry, upset gamblers. He saw Jerry and Billy against the side of the truck, watching him and Ivy drive by, and he could hear Mrs. Brill's high-pitched voice protesting the indignity of it all. When they were safely past he pulled up again and turned back for a last look through the rear window. Ivy was looking back also, a worried frown creasing her forehead.

She turned away to study Jack's face. It was inscrutably solemn. "I guess . . . I guess trucks aren't supposed to use these roads at night," she said.

"I guess not," he agreed, turning back to her.

"What will you do?"

He started the car up slowly before putting his arm back around her. "First," he said, "we head for the nearest phone and I call the lawyers."

She nodded.

"Then I make a stop to pick something up." He glanced down at her, an easy pressure resting on his arm and shoulder.

"What?"

"Uh-uh," he said, shaking his head. "Don't be a prying female."

She looked up and wrinkled her nose at him. "Okay," she said.

"And then . . ."

"Then?" she asked softly.

"Then we go home."

The police vans passed them on the road, three large ones, heading for the truck, and Ivy followed them with her eyes until they were passed. Jack pointed the car toward the city and stopped at the first gas station to call the lawyers. He was gone a long time and Ivy leaned her head back against the seat and was sleeping when he returned. Her tension was gone now, and she slept with a hand tucked lightly beneath her chin.

He studied her carefully, gently covered her with his jacket and let her sleep. He whistled softly under his breath, heading out. She woke up briefly once and moved closer to him, her eyes shutting almost immediately; she was still asleep when he stopped on Fifty-fourth Street.

Jack parked across from the apartment building and gently shook her awake. She made a small protesting noise, opening her eyes slowly, smiling when she saw him and moving into the comfort of his arms. He held her lightly and toyed with her ear until she sat up and realized where they were. The overnight case in one hand, he guided her across the street and headed for the elevator.

They walked across the silent hall; Jack locked the apartment door after them.

"Will you go to jail?" she asked suddenly.

"Not very likely. But if I do, you'll bring me cookies, right?"

She nodded happily.

"Here," he said. "And take *care* of this one."

Ivy held in both hands, the little ashtray he had stopped for at the Japanese restaurant, turning it over and over. A soft, warm feeling rose in waves from a small point deep inside and threatened to drown her. Her eyes were shining as they told him what he wanted to know.

"Just one more thing we have to clear up," he said seriously.

"What's that?"

"What have you got against West Indians?"